The Surgeon's Daughter

CHRONICLES OF THE CANONGATE

Sic Itur Ad Astra.

SIR WALTER SCOTT

ferenity
Publishers, LLC
ROCKVILLE, MARYLAND
2012

ISBN: 978-1-61242-808-6

Published by Serenity Publishers
An Arc Manor Company
P. O. Box 10339
Rockville, MD 20849-0339
www.SerenityPublishers.com

Printed in the United States of America/United Kingdom

Contents

Introduction

(1831)

The tale of the Surgeon's Daughter formed part of the second series of Chronicles of the Canongate, published in 1827; but has been separated from the stories of the Highland Widow, &c., which it originally accompanied, and deferred to the close of this collection, for reasons which printers and publishers will understand, and which would hardly interest the general reader.

The Author has nothing to say now in reference to this little Novel, but that the principal incident on which it turns, was narrated to him one morning at breakfast by his worthy friend, Mr. Train, of Castle Douglas, in Galloway, whose kind assistance he has so often had occasion to acknowledge in the course of these prefaces; and that the military friend who is alluded to as having furnished him with some information as to Eastern matters, was Colonel James Ferguson of Huntly Burn, one of the sons of the venerable historian and philosopher of that name—which name he took the liberty of concealing under its Gaelic form of *Mac-Erries*.

ABBOTSFORD, *September* 1831.

○○○○○ ◆ ○○○○○

Appendix to Introduction

Mr. Train was requested by Sir Walter Scott to give him in writing the story as nearly as possible in the shape in which he had told it; but the following narrative, which he drew up accordingly, did not reach Abbotsford until July 1832.

In the old Stock of Fife, there was not perhaps an individual whose exertions were followed by consequences of such a remarkable nature as those of Davie Duff, popularly called "The Thane of Fife," who, from a very humble parentage, rose to fill one of the chairs of the magistracy of his native burgh. By industry and economy in early life, he obtained the means of erecting, solely on his own account, one of those ingenious manufactories for which Fifeshire is justly celebrated. From the day on which the industrious artisan first took his seat at the Council Board, he attended so much to the interests of the little privileged community, that civic honours were conferred on him as rapidly as the Set of the Royalty[1] could legally admit.

To have the right of walking to church on holy-days, preceded by a phalanx of halberdiers, in habiliments fashioned as in former times, seems, in the eyes of many a guild brother, to be a very enviable pitch of worldly grandeur. Few persons were ever more proud of civic honours than the Thane of Fife, but he knew well how to turn his political influence to the best account. The council, court, and other business of the burgh, occupied much of his time, which caused him to intrust the management of his manufactory to a near relation, whose name was D——, a young man of dissolute habits; but the Thane, seeing at last, that by continuing that extravagant person in that charge, his affairs would, in all probability, fall into a state of bankruptcy, applied to the member of Parliament for that district to obtain a situation for his relation in

---

1   The Constitution of the Borough.

the civil department of the state. The knight, whom it is here unnecessary to name, knowing how effectually the Thane ruled the little burgh, applied in the proper quarter, and actually obtained an appointment for D—in the civil service of the East India Company.

A respectable surgeon, whose residence was in a neighbouring village, had a beautiful daughter named Emma, who had long been courted by D—. Immediately before his departure to India, as a mark of mutual affection, they exchanged miniatures, taken by an eminent artist in Fife, and each set in a locket, for the purpose of having the object of affection always in view.

The eyes of the old Thane were now turned towards Hindostan with much anxiety; but his relation had not long arrived in that distant quarter of the globe before he had the satisfaction of receiving a letter, conveying the welcome intelligence of his having taken possession of his new station in a large frontier town of the Company's dominions, and that great emoluments were attached to the situation; which was confirmed by several subsequent communications of the most gratifying description to the old Thane, who took great pleasure in spreading the news of the reformed habits and singular good fortune of his intended heir. None of all his former acquaintances heard with such joy the favourable report of the successful adventurer in the East, as did the fair and accomplished daughter of the village surgeon; but his previous character caused her to keep her own correspondence with him secret from her parents, to whom even the circumstance of her being acquainted with D—was wholly unknown, till her father received a letter from him, in which he assured him of his attachment to Emma long before his departure from Fife; that having been so happy as to gain her affections, he would have made her his wife before leaving his native country, had he then had the means of supporting her in a suitable rank through life; and that, having it now in his power to do so, he only waited the consent of her parents to fulfil the vow he had formerly made.

The Doctor having a large family, with a very limited income to support them, and understanding that D—had at last become a person of sober and industrious habits, he gave his consent, in which Emma's mother fully concurred.

Aware of the straitened circumstances of the Doctor, D—remitted a sum of money to complete at Edinburgh Emma's Oriental education, and fit her out in her journey to India; she was to embark at Sheerness, on board one of the Company's ships, for a port in India, at which place, he said, he would wait her arrival, with a retinue suited to a person of his rank in society.

Emma set out from her father's house just in time to secure a passage, as proposed by her intended husband, accompanied by her only brother, who, on their arrival at Sheerness, met one C—, an old schoolfellow, captain of the ship by which Emma was to proceed to India.

It was the particular desire of the Doctor that his daughter should be committed to the care of that gentleman, from the time of her leaving the shores of Britain, till the intended marriage ceremony was duly performed on her arrival in India; a charge that was frankly undertaken by the generous sea-captain.

On the arrival of the fleet at the appointed port, D—, with a large cavalcade of mounted Pindarees, was, as expected, in attendance, ready to salute Emma on landing, and to carry her direct into the interior of the country. C—, who had made several voyages to the shores of Hindostan, knowing something of Hindoo manners and customs, was surprised to see a private individual in the Company's service with so many attendants; and when D— declined having the marriage ceremony performed according to the rites of the Church, till he returned to the place of his abode, C—, more and more confirmed in his suspicion that all was not right, resolved not to part with Emma till he had fulfilled, in the most satisfactory manner, the promise he had made before leaving England, of giving her duly away in marriage. Not being able by her entreaties to alter the resolution of D—, Emma solicited her protector C—to accompany her to the place of her intended destination, to which he most readily agreed, taking with him as many of his crew as he deemed sufficient to ensure the safe custody of his innocent protege, should any attempt be made to carry her away by force.

Both parties journeyed onwards till they arrived at a frontier town, where a native Rajah was waiting the arrival of the fair maid of Fife, with whom he had fallen deeply in love, from seeing her miniature likeness in the possession of D—, to whom he had paid a large sum of money for the original, and had only intrusted him to convey her in state to the seat of his government.

No sooner was this villanous action of D—known to C—, than he communicated the whole particulars to the commanding officer of a regiment of Scotch Highlanders that happened to be quartered in that part of India, begging at the same time, for the honour of Caledonia, and protection of injured innocence, that he would use the means in his power, of resisting any attempt that might be made by the native chief to wrest from their hands the virtuous female who had been so shamefully decoyed from her native country by the worst of mankind. Honour occupies too large a space in the heart of the Gael to resist such a call of humanity.

The Rajah, finding his claim was not to be acceded to, and resolving to enforce the same, assembled his troops, and attacked with great fury the place where the affrighted Emma was for a time secured by her countrymen, who fought in her defence with all their native valour, which at length so overpowered their assailants, that they were forced to retire in every direction, leaving behind many of their slain, among whom was found the mangled corpse of the perfidious D—.

C—was immediately afterwards married to Emma, and my informant assured me he saw them many years afterwards, living happily together in the county of Kent, on the fortune bequeathed by the "Thane of Fife."

J. T.
CASTLE DOUGLAS,
July, 1832.

Mr. Croftangry's Preface

Indite, my muse indite,
Subpoena'd is thy lyre,
The praises to requite
Which rules of court require.

PROBATIONARY ODES.

The concluding a literary undertaking, in whole or in part, is, to the inexperienced at least, attended with an irritating titillation, like that which attends on the healing of a wound—a prurient impatience, in short, to know what the world in general, and friends in particular, will say to our labours. Some authors, I am told, profess an oyster-like indifference upon this subject; for my own part, I hardly believe in their sincerity. Others may acquire it from habit; but, in my poor opinion, a neophyte like myself must be for a long time incapable of such *sang froid*.

Frankly, I was ashamed to feel how childishly I felt on the occasion. No person could have said prettier things than myself upon the importance of stoicism concerning the opinion of others, when their applause or censure refers to literary character only; and I had determined to lay my work before the public, with the same unconcern with which the ostrich lays her eggs in the sand, giving herself no farther trouble concerning the incubation, but leaving to the atmosphere to bring forth the young, or otherwise, as the climate shall serve. But though an ostrich in theory, I became in practice a poor hen, who has no sooner made her deposit, but she runs cackling about, to call the attention of every one to the wonderful work which she has performed.

As soon as I became possessed of my first volume, neatly stitched up and boarded, my sense of the necessity of communicating with some one became ungovernable. Janet was inexorable, and seemed already to have tired of my literary confidence; for whenever I drew near the subject, after evading it as long as she could, she made, under some pretext or other, a bodily retreat to the kitchen or the cockloft, her own peculiar and inviolate domains. My publisher would have been a natural resource; but he understands his business too well, and follows it too closely, to desire to enter into literary discussions, wisely considering, that he who has to sell books has seldom leisure to read them. Then my acquaintance, now that I have lost Mrs. Bethune Baliol, are of that distant and accidental kind, to whom I had not face enough to communicate the nature of my uneasiness, and who probably would only have laughed at me had I made any attempt to interest them in my labours.

Reduced thus to a sort of despair, I thought of my friend and man of business, Mr. Fairscribe. His habits, it was true, were not likely to render him indulgent to light literature, and, indeed, I had more than once noticed his daughters, and especially my little songstress, whip into her reticule what looked very like a circulating library volume, as soon as her father entered the room. Still he was not only my assured, but almost my only friend, and I had little doubt that he would take an interest in the volume for the sake of the author, which the work itself might fail to inspire. I sent him, therefore, the book, carefully sealed up, with an intimation that I requested the favour of his opinion upon the contents, of which I affected to talk in the depreciatory style, which calls for point-blank contradiction, if your correspondent possess a grain of civility.

This communication took place on a Monday, and I daily expected (what I was ashamed to anticipate by volunteering my presence, however sure of a welcome) an invitation to eat an egg, as was my friend's favourite phrase, or a card to drink tea with Misses Fairscribe, or a provocation to breakfast, at least, with my hospitable friend and benefactor, and to talk over the contents of my enclosure. But the hours and days passed on from Monday till Saturday, and I had no acknowledgment whatever that my packet had reached its destination. "This is very unlike my good friend's punctuality," thought I; and having again and again vexed James, my male attendant, by a close examination concerning the time, place, and delivery, I had only to strain my imagination to conceive reasons for my friend's silence. Sometimes I thought that his opinion of the work had proved so unfavourable that he was averse to hurt my feelings by communicating it—sometimes, that, escaping his hands to whom it was destined, it had found its way into his writing-chamber, and was become the subject of criticism to his smart clerks and conceited apprentices. "'Sdeath!" thought I, "if I were sure of this, I would"—

"And what would you do?" said Reason, after a few moment's reflection. "You are ambitious of introducing your book into every writing and reading-chamber in Edinburgh, and yet you take fire at the thoughts of its being criticised by Mr. Fairscribe's young people? Be a little consistent—for shame!"

"I will be consistent," said I, doggedly; "but for all that, I will call on Mr. Fairscribe this evening."

I hastened my dinner, donn'd my great-coat (for the evening threatened rain,) and went to Mr. Fairscribe's house. The old domestic opened the door cautiously, and before I asked the question, said, "Mr. Fairscribe is at home, sir; but it is Sunday night." Recognising, however, my face and voice, he opened the door wider, admitted me, and conducted me to the parlour, where I found Mr. Fairscribe and the rest of his family engaged in listening to a sermon by the late Mr. Walker of Edinburgh,[2] which was read by Miss Catherine with unusual distinctness, simplicity, and judgment. Welcomed as a friend of the house, I had nothing for it but to take my seat quietly, and making a virtue of necessity, endeavour to derive my share of the benefit arising from an excellent sermon. But I am afraid Mr. Walker's force of logic and precision of expression were somewhat lost upon me. I was sensible I had chosen an improper time to disturb Mr. Fairscribe, and when the discourse was ended, I rose to take my leave, somewhat hastily, I believe. "A cup of tea, Mr. Croftangry?" said the young lady. "You will wait and take part of a Presbyterian supper?" said Mr. Fairscribe.—"Nine o'clock—I make it a point of keeping my father's hours on Sunday at e'en. Perhaps Dr.—(naming an excellent clergyman) may look in."

I made my apology for declining his invitation; and I fancy my unexpected appearance, and hasty retreat, had rather surprised my friend, since, instead of accompanying me to the door, he conducted me into his own apartment.

"What is the matter," he said, "Mr. Croftangry? This is not a night for secular business, but if any thing sudden or extraordinary has happened"—

"Nothing in the world," said I, forcing myself upon confession, as the best way of clearing myself out of the scrape,—"only—only I sent you a little parcel, and as you are so regular in acknowledging letters and communications, I—I thought it might have miscarried—that's all."

My friend laughed heartily, as if he saw into and enjoyed my motives and my confusion. "Safe?—it came safe enough," he said. "The wind of the world always blows its vanities into haven. But this is the end of the session, when I have little time to read any thing printed except Inner-House papers; yet if you will take your kail with us next Saturday, I will glance over your work, though I am sure I am no competent judge of such matters."

With this promise I was fain to take my leave, not without half persuading myself that if once the phlegmatic lawyer began my lucubrations, he would not be able to rise from them till he had finished the perusal, nor to endure an interval betwixt his reading the last page, and requesting an interview with the author.

No such marks of impatience displayed themselves. Time, blunt or keen, as my friend Joanna says, swift or leisurely, held his course; and on the

---

2   Robert Walker, the colleague and rival of Dr. Hugh Blair, in St. Giles's Church Edinburgh

appointed Saturday, I was at the door precisely as it struck four. The dinner hour, indeed, was five punctually; but what did I know but my friend might want half an hour's conversation with me before that time? I was ushered into an empty drawing-room, and, from a needle-book and work-basket hastily abandoned, I had some reason to think I interrupted my little friend, Miss Katie, in some domestic labour more praiseworthy than elegant. In this critical age, filial piety must hide herself in a closet, if she has a mind to darn her father's linen.

Shortly after, I was the more fully convinced that I had been too early an intruder when a wench came to fetch away the basket, and recommend to my courtesies a red and green gentleman in a cage, who answered all my advances by croaking out, "You're a fool—you're a fool, I tell you!" until, upon my word, I began to think the creature was in the right. At last my friend arrived, a little overheated. He had been taking a turn at golf, to prepare him for "colloquy sublime." And wherefore not? since the game, with its variety of odds, lengths, bunkers, tee'd balls, and so on, may be no inadequate representation of the hazards attending literary pursuits. In particular, those formidable buffets, which make one ball spin through the air like a rifle-shot, and strike another down into the very earth it is placed upon, by the mal-adroitness, or the malicious purpose of the player—what are they but parallels to the favourable or depreciating notices of the reviewers, who play at golf with the publications of the season, even as Altisidora, in her approach to the gates of the infernal regions, saw the devils playing at racket with the new books of Cervantes' days.

Well, every hour has its end. Five o'clock came, and my friend, with his daughters, and his handsome young son, who, though fairly buckled to the desk, is every now and then looking over his shoulder at a smart uniform, set seriously about satisfying the corporeal wants of nature; I, stimulated by a nobler appetite after fame, wished that the touch of a magic wand could, without all the ceremony of picking and choosing, carving and slicing, masticating and swallowing, have transported a *quantum sufficit* of the good things on my friend's hospitable board, into the stomachs of those who surrounded it, to be there at leisure converted into chyle, while their thoughts were turned on higher matters. At length all was over. But the young ladies sat still, and talked of the music of the Freischutz, for nothing else was then thought of; so we discussed the wild hunter's song, and the tame hunter's song, &c. &c., in all which my young friends were quite at home. Luckily for me, all this horning and hooping drew on some allusion to the Seventh Hussars, which gallant regiment, I observe, is a more favourite theme with both Miss Catherine and her brother than with my old friend, who presently looked at his watch, and said something significantly to Mr. James about office hours. The youth got up with the ease of a youngster that would be thought a man of fashion rather than of business, and endeavoured, with some success, to walk out of the room, as if the locomotion was entirely voluntary; Miss Catherine and her sisters left us at the same time, and now, thought I, my trial comes on.

Reader, did you ever, in the course of your life, cheat the courts of justice and lawyers, by agreeing to refer a dubious and important question to the decision of a mutual friend? If so, you may have remarked the relative change which the arbiter undergoes in your estimation, when raised, though by your own free choice, from an ordinary acquaintance, whose opinions were of as little consequence to you as yours to him, into a superior personage, on whose decision your fate must depend *pro tanto*, as my friend Mr. Fairscribe would say. His looks assume a mysterious if not a minatory expression; his hat has a loftier air, and his wig, if he wears one, a more formidable buckle.

I felt, accordingly, that my good friend Fairscribe, on the present occasion, had acquired something of a similar increase of consequence. But a week since, he had, in my opinion, been indeed an excellent-meaning man, perfectly competent to every thing within his own profession, but immured, at the same time, among its forms and technicalities, and as incapable of judging of matters of taste as any mighty Goth whatsoever, of or belonging to the ancient Senate-House of Scotland. But what of that? I had made him my judge by my own election; and I have often observed, that an idea of declining such a reference, on account of his own consciousness of incompetency, is, as it perhaps ought to be, the last which occurs to the referee himself. He that has a literary work subjected to his judgment by the author, immediately throws his mind into a critical attitude, though the subject be one which he never before thought of. No doubt the author is well qualified to select his own judge, and why should the arbiter whom he has chosen doubt his own talents for condemnation or acquittal, since he has been doubtless picked out by his friend, from his indubitable reliance on their competence? Surely, the man who wrote the production is likely to know the person best qualified to judge of it.

Whilst these thoughts crossed my brain, I kept my eyes fixed on my good friend, whose motions appeared unusually tardy to me, while he ordered a bottle of particular claret, decanted it with scrupulous accuracy with his own hand, caused his old domestic to bring a saucer of olives, and chips of toasted bread, and thus, on hospitable thoughts intent, seemed to me to adjourn the discussion which I longed to bring on, yet feared to precipitate.

"He is dissatisfied," thought I, "and is ashamed to show it, afraid doubtless of hurting my feelings. What had I to do to talk to him about any thing save charters and sasines?—Stay, he is going to begin."

"We are old fellows now, Mr. Croftangry," said my landlord; "scarcely so fit to take a poor quart of claret between us, as we would have been in better days to take a pint, in the old Scottish liberal acceptation of the phrase.

Maybe you would have liked me to have kept James to help us. But if it is not a holyday or so, I think it is best he should observe office hours."

Here the discourse was about to fall. I relieved it by saying, Mr. James was at the happy time of life, when he had better things to do than to sit over the bottle. "I suppose," said I, "your son is a reader."

"Um—yes—James may be called a reader in a sense; but I doubt there is little solid in his studies—poetry and plays, Mr. Croftangry, all nonsense—they set his head a-gadding after the army, when he should be minding his business."

"I suppose, then, that romances do not find much more grace in your eyes than dramatic and poetical compositions?"

"Deil a bit, deil a bit, Mr. Croftangry, nor historical productions either. There is too much fighting in history, as if men only were brought into this world to send one another out of it. It nourishes false notions of our being, and chief and proper end, Mr. Croftangry."

Still all this was general, and I became determined to bring our discourse to a focus. "I am afraid, then, I have done very ill to trouble you with my idle manuscripts, Mr. Fairscribe; but you must do me the justice to remember, that I had nothing better to do than to amuse myself by writing the sheets I put into your hands the other day. I may truly plead—

'I left no calling for this idle trade.'"

"I cry your mercy, Mr. Croftangry," said my old friend, suddenly recollecting—"yes, yes, I have been very rude; but I had forgotten entirely that you had taken a spell yourself at that idle man's trade."

"I suppose," replied I, "you, on your side, have been too *busy* a man to look at my poor Chronicles?"

"No, no," said my friend, "I am not so bad as that neither. I have read them bit by bit, just as I could get a moment's time, and I believe, I shall very soon get through them."

"Well, my good friend?" said I, interrogatively.

And "*Well*, Mr. Croftangry," cried he, "I really think you have got over the ground very tolerably well. I have noted down here two or three bits of things, which I presume to be errors of the press, otherwise it might be alleged, perhaps, that you did not fully pay that attention to the grammatical rules, which one would desire to see rigidly observed."

I looked at my friend's notes, which, in fact, showed, that in one or two grossly obvious passages, I had left uncorrected such solecisms in grammar.

"Well, well, I own my fault; but, setting apart these casual errors, how do you like the matter and the manner of what I have been writing, Mr. Fairscribe?"

"Why," said my friend, pausing, with more grave and important hesitation than I thanked him for, "there is not much to be said against the manner. The style is terse and intelligible, Mr. Croftangry, very intelligible; and that I consider as the first point in every thing that is intended to be understood. There are, indeed, here and there some flights and fancies, which I comprehended with difficulty; but I got to your meaning at last. There are people that are like ponies; their judgments cannot go fast, but they go sure."

"That is a pretty clear proposition, my friend; but then how did you like the meaning when you did get at it? or was that like some ponies, too difficult to catch, and, when caught, not worth the trouble?"

"I am far from saying that, my dear sir, in respect it would be downright uncivil; but since you ask my opinion, I wish you could have thought about something more appertaining to civil policy, than all this bloody work about shooting and dirking, and downright hanging. I am told it was the Germans who first brought in such a practice of choosing their heroes out of the Porteous Roll;[3] but, by my faith, we are like to be upsides with them. The first was, as I am credibly informed, Mr. Scolar, as they call him; a scholar-like piece of work he has made of it, with his robbers and thieves."

"Schiller," said I, "my dear sir, let it be Schiller."

"Schiller, or what you like," said Mr. Fairscribe; "I found the book where I wish I had found a better one, and that is, in Kate's work-basket. I sat down, and, like an old fool, began to read; but there, I grant, you have the better of Schiller, Mr. Croftangry."

"I should be glad, my dear sir, that you really think I have *approached* that admirable author; even your friendly partiality ought not to talk of my having *excelled* him."

"But I do say you have excelled him, Mr. Croftangry, in a most material particular. For surely a book of amusement should be something that one can take up and lay down at pleasure; and I can say justly, I was never at the least loss to put aside these sheets of yours when business came in the way. But, faith, this Schiller, sir, does not let you off so easily. I forgot one appointment on particular business, and I wilfully broke through another, that I might stay at home and finish his confounded book, which, after all, is about two brothers, the greatest rascals I ever heard of. The one, sir, goes near to murder his own father, and the other (which you would think still stranger) sets about to debauch his own wife."

"I find, then, Mr. Fairscribe, that you have no taste for the romance of real life—no pleasure in contemplating those spirit-rousing impulses, which force men of fiery passions upon great crimes and great virtues?"

"Why, as to that, I am not just so sure. But then to mend the matter," continued the critic, "you have brought in Highlanders into every story, as if you were going back again, *velis et remis*, into the old days of Jacobitism. I must speak my plain mind, Mr. Croftangry. I cannot tell what innovations in Kirk and State may now be proposed, but our fathers were friends to both, as

---

3   List of criminal indictments, so termed in Scotland.

they were settled at the glorious Revolution, and liked a tartan plaid as little as they did a white surplice. I wish to Heaven, all this tartan fever bode well to the Protestant succession and the Kirk of Scotland."

"Both too well settled, I hope, in the minds of the subject," said I, "to be affected by old remembrances, on which we look back as on the portraits of our ancestors, without recollecting, while we gaze on them, any of the feuds by which the originals were animated while alive. But most happy should I be to light upon any topic to supply the place of the Highlands, Mr. Fairscribe. I have been just reflecting that the theme is becoming a little exhausted, and your experience may perhaps supply"—

"Ha, ha, ha!—*my* experience supply!" interrupted Mr. Fairscribe, with a laugh of derision;—"why, you might as well ask my son James's experience to supply a case" about thirlage. No, no, my good friend, I have lived by the law, and in the law, all my life; and when you seek the impulses that make soldiers desert and shoot their sergeants and corporals, and Highland drovers dirk English graziers, to prove themselves men of fiery passions, it is not to a man like me you should come. I could tell you some tricks of my own trade, perhaps, and a queer story or two of estates that have been lost and recovered. But, to tell you the truth, I think you might do with your Muse of Fiction, as you call her, as many an honest man does with his own sons in flesh and blood."

"And how is that, my dear sir?"

"Send her to India, to be sure. That is the true place for a Scot to thrive in; and if you carry your story fifty years back, as there is nothing to hinder you, you will find as much shooting and stabbing there as ever was in the wild Highlands. If you want rogues, as they are so much in fashion with you, you have that gallant caste of adventurers, who laid down their consciences at the Cape of Good Hope as they went out to India, and forgot to take them up again when they returned. Then, for great exploits, you have in the old history of India, before Europeans were numerous there, the most wonderful deeds, done by the least possible means, that perhaps the annals of the world can afford."

"I know it," said I, kindling at the ideas his speech inspired. "I remember in the delightful pages of Orme, the interest which mingles in his narratives, from the very small number of English which are engaged. Each officer of a regiment becomes known to you by name, nay, the non-commissioned officers and privates acquire an individual share of interest. They are distinguished among the natives like the Spaniards among the Mexicans. What do I say? They are like Homer's demigods among the warring mortals. Men, like Clive and Caillaud, influenced great events, like Jove himself. Inferior officers are like Mars or Neptune; and the sergeants and corporals might well pass for demigods. Then the various religious costumes, habits, and manners of the people of Hindustan,—the patient Hindhu, the warlike Rajahpoot, the haughty Moslemah, the savage and vindictive Malay—Glorious and un-bounded subjects! The only objection is, that I have never been there, and know nothing at all about them."

"Nonsense, my good friend. You will tell us about them all the better that you know nothing of what you are saying; and come, we'll finish the bottle, and when Katie (her sisters go to the assembly) has given us tea, she will tell you the outline of the story of poor Menie Gray, whose picture you will see in the drawing-room, a distant relation of my father's, who had, however, a handsome part of cousin Menie's succession. There are none living that can be hurt by the story now, though it was thought best to smother it up at the time, as indeed even the whispers about it led poor cousin Menie to live very retired. I mind her well when a child. There was something very gentle, but rather tiresome, about poor cousin Menie."

When we came into the drawing-room, my friend pointed to a picture which I had before noticed, without, however, its having attracted more than a passing look; now I regarded it with more attention. It was one of those por-traits of the middle of the eighteenth century, in which artists endeavoured to conquer the stiffness of hoops and brocades; by throwing a fancy drapery around the figure, with loose folds like a mantle or dressing gown, the stays, however, being retained, and the bosom displayed in a manner which shows that our mothers, like their daughters, were as liberal of their charms as the nature of the dress might permit. To this, the well-known style of the period, the features and form of the individual added, at first sight, little interest. It represented a handsome woman of about thirty, her hair wound simply about her head, her features regular, and her complexion fair. But on looking more closely, especially after having had a hint that the original had been the heroine of a tale, I could observe a melancholy sweetness in the countenance that seemed to speak of woes endured, and injuries sustained, with that res-ignation which women can and do sometimes display under the insults and ingratitude of those on whom they have bestowed their affections.

"Yes, she was an excellent and an ill-used woman," said Mr. Fairscribe, his eye fixed like mine on the picture—"She left our family not less, I dare say, than five thousand pounds, and I believe she died worth four times that sum; but it was divided among the nearest of kin, which was all fair."

"But her history, Mr. Fairscribe," said I—"to judge from her look, it must have been a melancholy one."

"You may say that, Mr. Croftangry. Melancholy enough, and extraordi-nary enough too—But," added he, swallowing in haste a cup of the tea which was presented to him, "I must away to my business—we cannot be gowfling all the morning, and telling old stories all the afternoon. Katie knows all the outs and the ins of cousin Menie's adventures as well as I do, and when she has given you the particulars, then I am at your service, to condescend more articulately upon dates or particulars."

Well, here was I, a gay old bachelor, left to hear a love tale from my young friend Katie Fairscribe, who, when she is not surrounded by a bevy of gallants, at which time, to my thinking, she shows less to advantage, is as pretty, well-behaved, and unaffected a girl as you see tripping the new walks of Prince's Street or Heriot Row. Old bachelorship so decided as mine has its privileges in such a *tete-a-tete*, providing you are, or can seem for the time, perfectly good-humoured and attentive, and do not ape the manners of your younger years, in attempting which you will only make yourself ridiculous. I don't pretend to be so indifferent to the company of a pretty young woman as was desired by the poet, who wished to sit beside his mistress—

—*"As unconcern'd as when*
    Her infant beauty could beget
Nor happiness nor pain."

On the contrary, I can look on beauty and innocence, as something of which I know and esteem the value, without the desire or hope to make them my own. A young lady can afford to talk with an old stager like me without either artifice or affectation; and we may maintain a species of friendship, the more tender, perhaps, because we are of different sexes, yet with which that distinction has very little to do.

Now, I hear my wisest and most critical neighbour remark, "Mr. Croftangry is in the way of doing a foolish thing, He is well to pass—Old Fairscribe knows to a penny what he is worth, and Miss Katie, with all her airs, may like the old brass that buys the new pan. I thought Mr. Croftangry was looking very cadgy when he came in to play a rubber with us last night. Poor gentleman, I am sure I should be sorry to see him make a fool of himself."

Spare your compassion, dear madam, there is not the least danger. The *beaux yeux de ma casette* are not brilliant enough to make amends for the spectacles which must supply the dimness of my own. I am a little deaf, too, as you know to your sorrow when we are partners; and if I could get a nymph to marry me with all these imperfections, who the deuce would marry Janet McEvoy? and from Janet McEvoy Chrystal Croftangry will not part.

Miss Katie Fairscribe gave me the tale of Menie Gray with much taste and simplicity, not attempting to suppress the feelings, whether of grief or resentment, which justly and naturally arose from the circumstances of the tale. Her father afterwards confirmed the principal outlines of the story, and furnished me with some additional circumstances, which Miss Katie had suppressed or forgotten. Indeed, I have learned on this occasion, what old Lintot meant when he told Pope, that he used to propitiate the critics of importance, when he had a work in the press, by now and then letting them see a sheet of the blotted proof, or a few leaves of the original manuscript. Our mystery of authorship has something about it so fascinating, that if you admit any one, however little he may previously have been disposed to such studies, into your confidence, you will find that he considers himself as a party interested, and, if success follows, will think himself entitled to no inconsiderable share of the praise.

The reader has seen that no one could have been naturally less inter- ested than was my excellent friend Fairscribe in my lucubrations, when I first consulted him on the subject; but since he has contributed a subject to the work, he has become a most zealous coadjutor; and half-ashamed, I believe, yet half-proud of the literary stock-company, in which he has got a share, he never meets me without jogging my elbow, and dropping some mysterious hints, as, "I am saying—when will you give us any more of yon?"—or, "Yon's not a bad narrative—I like yon."

Pray Heaven the reader may be of his opinion.

The Surgeon's Daughter

CHAPTER 1

When fainting Nature call'd for aid,
*   And hovering Death prepared the blow,*
His vigorous remedy display'd
*   The power of art without the show;*
In Misery's darkest caverns known,
*   His useful care was ever nigh,*
Where hopeless Anguish pour'd his groan,
*   And lonely Want retired to die;*
No summons mock'd by cold delay,
*   No petty gains disclaim'd by pride,*
The modest wants of every day
*   The toil of every day supplied.*

SAMUEL JOHNSON.

The exquisitely beautiful portrait which the Rambler has painted of his friend Levett, well describes Gideon Gray, and many other village doctors, from whom Scotland reaps more benefit, and to whom she is perhaps more ungrateful than to any other class of men, excepting her schoolmasters.

Such a rural man of medicine is usually the inhabitant of some pretty borough or village, which forms the central point of his practice. But, besides attending to such cases as the village may afford, he is day and night at the service of every one who may command his assistance within a circle of forty miles in diameter, untraversed by roads in many directions, and including moors, mountains, rivers, and lakes. For late and dangerous journeys through an inaccessible country for services of the most essential kind, rendered at the expense, or risk at least, of his own health and life, the Scottish village doctor receives at best a very moderate recompense, often one which is totally inadequate, and very frequently none whatever. He has none of the ample resources proper to the brothers of the profession. in an English town. The burgesses of a Scottish borough are rendered, by their limited means of luxury, inaccessible to gout, surfeits, and all the comfortable chronic diseases which are attendant on wealth and indolence. Four years, or so, of abstemiousness, enable them to stand an election dinner; and there is no hope of broken heads among a score or two of quiet electors, who settle the business over a table. There the mothers of the state never make a point of pouring, in the course of every revolving year, a certain quantity of doctor's stuff through the bowels of their beloved children. Every old woman, from the Townhead to the Townfit, can prescribe a dose of salts, or spread a plaster; and it is only when a fever or a palsy renders matters serious, that the assistance of the doctor is invoked by his neighbours in the borough.

But still the man of science cannot complain of inactivity or want of practice. If he does not find patients at his door, he seeks them through a wide circle. Like the ghostly lover of Burger's Leonora, he mounts at midnight and traverses in darkness, paths which, to those less accustomed to them, seem formidable in daylight, through straits where the slightest aberration would plunge him into a morass, or throw him over a precipice, on to cabins which his horse might ride over without knowing they lay in his way, unless he happened to fall through the roofs. When he arrives at such a stately termination of his journey, where his services are required, either to bring a wretch into the world, or prevent one from leaving it, the scene of misery is often such, that, far from touching the hard-saved shillings which are gratefully offered to him, he bestows his medicines as well as his attendance—for charity. I have heard the celebrated traveller Mungo Park, who had experienced both courses of life, rather give the preference to travelling as a discoverer in Africa, than to wandering by night and day the wilds of his native land in the capacity of a country medical practitioner. He mentioned having once upon a time rode forty miles, sat up all night, and successfully assisted a woman under influence of the primitive curse, for which his sole remuneration was a roasted potato and a draught of buttermilk. But his was not the heart which grudged the labour that relieved human misery. In short, there is no creature in Scotland that works harder and is more poorly requited than the country doctor, unless perhaps it may be his horse. Yet the horse is, and indeed must be, hardy, active, and indefatigable, in spite of a rough coat and indifferent condition; and so you will often find in his master, under an unpromising and blunt exterior, professional skill and enthusiasm, intelligence, humanity, courage, and science.

Mr. Gideon Gray, surgeon in the village of Middlemas, situated in one of the midland counties of Scotland, led the rough, active, and ill-rewarded

course of life which we have endeavoured to describe. He was a man between forty and fifty, devoted to his profession, and of such reputation in
the medical world, that he had been more than once, as opportunities occurred, advised to exchange Middlemas and its meagre circle of practice, for
some of the larger towns in Scotland, or for Edinburgh itself. This advice he
had always declined. He was a plain blunt man, who did not love restraint,
and was unwilling to subject himself to that which was exacted in polite
society. He had not himself found out, nor had any friend hinted to him,
that a slight touch of the cynic, in manner and habits, gives the physician,
to the common eye, an air of authority which greatly tends to enlarge his
reputation. Mr. Gray, or, as the country people called him, Doctor Gray, (he
might hold the title by diploma for what I know, though he only claimed
the rank of Master of Arts,) had few wants, and these were amply supplied
by a professional income which generally approached two hundred pounds
a year, for which, upon an average, he travelled about five thousand miles
on horseback in the course of the twelve months. Nay, so liberally did this
revenue support himself and his ponies, called Pestle and Mortar, which he
exercised alternately, that he took a damsel to share it, Jean Watson, namely,
the cherry-cheeked daughter of an honest farmer, who being herself one of
twelve children who had been brought up on an income of fourscore pounds
a year, never thought there could be poverty in more than double the sum;
and looked on Gray, though now termed by irreverent youth the Old Doctor,
as a very advantageous match. For several years they had no children, and it
seemed as if Doctor Gray, who had so often assisted the efforts of the goddess Lucina, was never to invoke her in his own behalf. Yet his domestic roof
was, on a remarkable occasion, decreed to be the scene where the goddess's
art was required.

Late of an autumn evening three old women might be observed plying
their aged limbs through the single street of the village at Middlemas towards
the honoured door, which, fenced off from the vulgar causeway, was defended
by a broken paling, enclosing two slips of ground, half arable, half overrun
with an abortive attempt at shrubbery. The door itself was blazoned with the
name of Gideon Gray, M. A. Surgeon, &c. &c. Some of the idle young fellows, who had been a minute or two before loitering at the other end of the
street before the door of the alehouse, (for the pretended inn deserved no better name,) now accompanied the old dames with shouts of laughter, excited by
their unwonted agility; and with bets on the winner, as loudly expressed as if
they had been laid at the starting post of Middlemas races. "Half a mutchkin
on Luckie Simson!"—"Auld Peg Tamson against the field!"—"Mair speed,
Alison Jaup, ye'll tak the wind out of them yet!"—"Canny against the hill,
lasses, or we may have a burstern auld earline amang ye!" These, and a thousand such gibes, rent the air, without being noticed, or even heard, by the

anxious racers, whose object of contention seemed to be, which should first reach the Doctor's door.

"Guide us, Doctor, what can be the matter now?" said Mrs. Gray, whose character was that of a good-natured simpleton; "Here's Peg Tamson, Jean Simson, and Alison Jaup, running a race on the hie street of the burgh!"

The Doctor, who had but the moment before hung his wet great-coat before the fire, (for he was just dismounted from a long journey,) hastened down stairs, arguing some new occasion for his services, and happy, that, from, the character of the messengers, it was likely to be within burgh, and not landward.

He had just reached the door as Luckie Simson, one of the racers, arrived in the little area before it. She had got the start, and kept it, but at the expense, for the time, of her power of utterance; for when she came in presence of the Doctor, she stood blowing like a grampus, her loose toy flying back from her face, making the most violent effort to speak, but without the power of uttering a single intelligible word. Peg Thompson whipped in before her.

"The leddy, sir, the leddy!"

"Instant help, instant help!"—screeched rather than uttered, Alison Jaup; while Luckie Simson, who had certainly won the race, found words to claim the prize which had set them all in motion.

"And I hope, sir, you will recommend me to be the sick-nurse; I was here to bring you the tidings lang before ony o' thae lazy queans."

Loud were the counter-protestations of the two competitors, and loud the laugh of the idle *loons* who listened at a little distance.

"Hold your tongue, ye flyting fools," said the Doctor; "and you, ye idle rascals, if I come out among you." So saying, he smacked his long-lashed whip with great emphasis, producing much the effect of the celebrated *Quos ego* of Neptune in the first Æneid.—"And now," said the Doctor, "where, or who, is this lady?"

The question was scarce necessary; for a plain carriage, with four horses, came at a foot's pace towards the door of the Doctor's house, and the old women, now more at their ease, gave the Doctor to understand, that the gentleman thought the accommodation of the Swan Inn totally unfit for his lady's rank and condition, and had, by their advice, (each claiming the merit of the suggestion,) brought her here, to experience the hospitality of the *west room;*—a spare apartment, in which Doctor Gray occasionally accommodated such patients, as he desired to keep for a space of time under his own eye.

There were two persons only in the vehicle. The one, a gentleman in a riding dress, sprung out, and having received from the Doctor an assurance that the lady would receive tolerable accommodation in his house, he lent assistance to his companion to leave the carriage, and with great apparent satisfaction, saw her safely deposited in a decent sleeping apartment, and under the respectable charge of the Doctor and his lady, who assured him once more of every species of attention. To bind their promise more firmly, the stranger slipped a purse of twenty guineas (for this story chanced in the golden age) into the hand of the Doctor, as an earnest of the most liberal recompense, and requested he would spare no expense in providing all that was necessary or desirable for a person in the lady's condition, and for the helpless being to whom she might immediately be expected to give birth. He then said he would retire to the inn, where he begged a message might instantly acquaint him with the expected change in the lady's situation.

"She is of rank," he said, "and a foreigner; let no expense be spared. We designed to have reached Edinburgh, but were forced to turn off the road by an accident." Once more he said, "Let no expense be spared, and manage that she may travel as soon as possible."

"That," said the Doctor, "is past my control. Nature must not be hurried, and she avenges herself of every attempt to do so."

"But art," said the stranger, "can do much," and he proffered a second purse, which seemed as heavy as the first.

"Art," said the Doctor, "may be recompensed, but cannot be purchased. You have already paid me more than enough to take the utmost care I can of your lady; should I accept more money, it could only be for promising, by implication at least, what is beyond my power to perform. Every possible care shall be taken of your lady, and that affords the best chance of her being speedily able to travel. Now, go you to the inn, sir, for I may be instantly wanted, and we have not yet provided either an attendant for the lady, or a nurse for the child; but both shall be presently done."

"Yet a moment, Doctor—what languages do you understand?"

"Latin and French I can speak indifferently, and so as to be understood; and I read a little Italian."

"But no Portuguese or Spanish?" continued the stranger.

"No, sir."

"That is unlucky. But you may make her understand you by means of French. Take notice, you are to comply with her request in everything—if you want means to do so, you may apply to me."

"May I ask, sir, by what name the lady is to be"—

"It is totally indifferent," said the stranger, interrupting the question; "You shall know it at more leisure."

So saying, he threw his ample cloak about him, turning himself half round to assist the operation, with an air which the Doctor would have found it difficult to imitate, and walked down the street to the little inn. Here he paid and dismissed the postilions, and shut himself up in an apartment, ordering no one to be admitted till the Doctor should call.

The Doctor, when he returned to his patient's apartment, found his wife in great surprise, which, as is usual with persons of her character, was not unmixed with fear and anxiety.

"She cannot speak a word like a Christian being," said Mrs. Gray.

"I know it," said the Doctor.

"But she threeps to keep on a black fause-face, and skirls if we offer to take it away."

"Well then, let her wear it—What harm will it do?"

"Harm, Doctor!" Was ever honest woman brought to bed with a fause-face on?"

"Seldom, perhaps. But, Jean, my dear, those who are not quite honest must be brought to bed all the same as those who are, and we are not to endanger the poor thing's life by contradicting her whims at present."

Approaching the sick woman's bed, he observed that she indeed wore a thin silk mask, of the kind which do such uncommon service in the elder comedy; such as women of rank still wore in travelling, but certainly never in the situation of this poor lady. It would seem she had sustained importunity on the subject, for when she saw the Doctor, she put her hand to her face, as if she was afraid he would insist on pulling off the vizard.

He hastened to say, in tolerable French, that her will should be a law to them in every respect, and that she was at perfect liberty to wear the mask till it was her pleasure to lay it aside. She understood him; for she replied, by a very imperfect attempt, in the same language, to express her gratitude for the permission, as she seemed to regard it, of retaining her disguise.

The Doctor proceeded to other arrangements; and, for the satisfaction of those readers who may love minute information, we record, that Luckie Simson, the first in the race, carried as a prize the situation of sick-nurse beside the delicate patient; that Peg Thomson was permitted the privilege of recommending her good-daughter, Bet Jamieson, to be wet-nurse; and an *oe*, or grandchild, of Luckie Jaup was hired to assist in the increased drudgery of the family; the Doctor thus, like a practised minister, dividing among his trusty adherents such good things as fortune placed at his disposal.

About one in the morning the Doctor made his appearance at the Swan Inn, and acquainted the stranger gentleman, that he wished him joy of being the father of a healthy boy, and that the mother was, in the usual phrase, as well as could be expected.

The stranger heard the news with seeming satisfaction, and then exclaimed, "He must be christened, Doctor! he must be christened instantly!"

"There can be no hurry for that," said the Doctor.

"*We* think otherwise," said the stranger, cutting his argument short. "I am a Catholic, Doctor, and as I may be obliged to leave this place before the lady is able to travel, I desire to see my child received into the pale of the Church. There is, I understand, a Catholic priest in this wretched place?"

"There is a Catholic gentleman, sir, Mr. Goodriche, who is reported to be in orders."

"I commend your caution, Doctor," said the stranger; "it is dangerous to be too positive on any subject. I will bring that same Mr. Goodriche to your house to-morrow."

Gray hesitated for a moment. "I am a Presbyterian Protestant, sir," he said, "a friend to the constitution as established in Church and State, as I have a good right, having drawn his Majesty's pay, God bless him, for four years, as surgeon's mate in the Cameronian regiment, as my regimental Bible and commission can testify. But although I be bound especially to abhor all trafficking or trinketing with Papists, yet I will not stand in the way of a tender conscience. Sir, you may call with Mr. Goodriche, when you please, at my house; and undoubtedly, you being, as I suppose, the father of the child, you will arrange matters as you please; only, I do not desire to be though an abettor or countenancer of any part of the Popish ritual."

"Enough, sir," said the stranger haughtily, "we understand each other."

The next day he appeared at the Doctor's house with Mr. Goodriche, and two persons understood to belong to that reverend gentleman's communion. The party were shut up in an apartment with the infant, and it may be presumed that the solemnity of baptism was administered to the unconscious being, thus strangely launched upon the world. When the priest and witnesses had retired, the strange gentleman informed Mr. Gray, that, as the lady had been pronounced unfit for travelling for several days, he was himself about to leave the neighbourhood, but would return thither in the space of ten days, when he hoped to find his companion able to leave it.

"And by what name are we to call the child and mother?"

"The infant's name is Richard."

"But it must have some sirname—so must the lady—She cannot reside in my house, yet be without a name."

"Call them by the name of your town here—Middlemas, I think it is?"

"Yes, sir."

"Well, Mrs. Middlemas is the name of the mother, and Richard Middlemas of the child—and I am Matthew Middlemas, at your service. This," he continued, "will provide Mrs. Middlemas in every thing she may wish to possess—or assist her in case of accidents." With that he placed L100 in Mr. Gray's hand, who rather scrupled receiving it, saying, "He supposed the lady was qualified to be her own purse-bearer."

"The worst in the world, I assure you, Doctor," replied the stranger. "If she wished to change that piece of paper, she would scarce know how many guineas she should receive for it. No, Mr. Gray, I assure you you will find

Mrs. Middleton—Middlemas—what did I call her—as ignorant of the affairs of this world as any one you have met with in your practice: So you will please to be her treasurer and administrator for the time, as for a patient that is incapable to look after her own affairs."

This was spoke, as it struck Dr. Gray, in rather a haughty and supercilious manner. The words intimated nothing in themselves, more than the same desire of preserving incognito, which might be gathered from all the rest of the stranger's conduct; but the manner seemed to say, "I am not a person to be questioned by any one—what I say must be received without comment, how little soever you may believe or understand it." It strengthened Gray in his opinion, that he had before him a case either of seduction, or of private marriage, betwixt persons of the very highest rank; and the whole bearing, both of the lady and the gentleman, confirmed his suspicions. It was not in his nature to be troublesome or inquisitive, but he could not fail to see that the lady wore no marriage-ring; and her deep sorrow, and perpetual tremor, seemed to indicate an unhappy creature, who had lost the protection of parents, without acquiring a legitimate right to that of a husband. He was therefore somewhat anxious when Mr. Middlemas, after a private conference of some length with the lady, bade him farewell. It is true, he assured him of his return within ten days, being the very shortest space which Gray could be prevailed upon to assign for any prospect of the lady being moved with safety.

"I trust in Heaven that he will return," said Gray to himself, "but there is too much mystery about all this, for the matter being a plain and well-meaning transaction. If he intends to treat this poor thing, as many a poor girl has been used before, I hope that my house will not be the scene in which he chooses to desert her. The leaving the money has somewhat a suspicious aspect, and looks as if my friend were in the act of making some compromise with his conscience. Well—I must hope the best. Meantime, my path plainly is to do what I can for the poor lady's benefit."

Mr. Gray visited his patient shortly after Mr. Middlemas's departure—as soon, indeed, as he could be admitted. He found her in violent agitation. Gray's experience dictated the best mode of relief and tranquillity. He caused her infant to be brought to her. She wept over it for a long time, and the violence of her agitation subsided under the influence of parental feelings, which, from her appearance of extreme youth, she must have experienced for the first time.

The observant physician could, after this paroxysm, remark that his patient's mind was chiefly occupied in computing the passage of the time, and anticipating the period when the return of her husband—if husband he was—might be expected. She consulted almanacks, enquired concerning distances, though so cautiously as to make it evident she desired to give no indication of the direction of her companion's journey, and repeatedly compared, her watch with those of others; exercising, it was evident, all that delusive species of mental arithmetic by which mortals attempt to accelerate the passage of Time while they calculate his progress. At other times she wept anew over her child, which was by all judges pronounced as goodly an infant as needed to be seen; and Gray sometimes observed that she murmured sentences to the unconscious infant, not only the words, but the very sound and accents of which were strange to him, and which, in particular, he knew not to be Portuguese.

Mr. Goodriche, the Catholic priest, demanded access to her upon one occasion. She at first declined his visit, but afterwards received it, under the idea, perhaps, that he might have news from Mr. Middlemas, as he called himself. The interview was a very short one, and the priest left the lady's apartment in displeasure, which his prudence could scarce disguise from Mr. Gray. He never returned, although the lady's condition would have made his attentions and consolations necessary, had she been a member of the Catholic Church.

Our Doctor began at length to suspect his fair guest was a Jewess, who had yielded up her person and affections to one of a different religion; and the peculiar style of her beautiful countenance went to enforce this opinion. The circumstance made no difference to Gray, who saw only her distress and desolation, and endeavoured to remedy both to the utmost of his power. He was, however, desirous to conceal it from his wife, and the others around the sick person, whose prudence and liberality of thinking might be more justly doubted. He therefore so regulated her diet, that she could not be either offended, or brought under suspicion, by any of the articles forbidden by the Mosaic law being presented to her. In other respects than what concerned her health or convenience, he had but little intercourse with her.

The space passed within which the stranger's return to the borough had been so anxiously expected by his female companion. The disappointment occasioned by his non-arrival was manifested in the convalescent by inquietude, which was at first mingled with peevishness, and afterwards with doubt and fear. When two or three days had passed without message or letter of any kind, Gray himself became anxious, both on his own account and the poor lady's, lest the stranger should have actually entertained the idea of deserting this defenceless and probably injured woman. He longed to have some communication with her, which might enable him to judge what enquiries could be made, or what else was most fitting to be done. But so imperfect was the poor young woman's knowledge of the French language, and perhaps so unwilling she herself to throw any light on her situation, that every attempt of this kind proved abortive. When Gray asked questions concerning any subject which appeared to approach to explanation, he observed she usually answered him by shaking her head, in token of not understanding what he said; at other times by silence and with tears, and sometimes referring him to *Monsieur*.

For *Monsieur's* arrival, then, Gray began to become very impatient, as that which alone could put an end to a disagreeable species of mystery, which the good company of the borough began now to make the principal subject of their gossip; some blaming Gray for taking foreign *landloupers*[4] into his house, on the subject of whose morals the most serious doubts might be entertained; others envying the "bonny hand" the doctor was like to make of it, by having disposal of the wealthy stranger's travelling funds; a circumstance which could not be well concealed from the public, when the honest man's expenditure for trifling articles of luxury came far to exceed its ordinary bounds.

The conscious probity of the honest Doctor enabled him to despise this sort of tittle-tattle, though the secret knowledge of its existence could not be agreeable to him. He went his usual rounds with his usual perseverance, and waited with patience until time should throw light on the subject and history of his lodger. It was now the fourth week after her confinement, and the recovery of the stranger might be considered as perfect, when Gray, returning from one of his ten-mile visits, saw a post-chaise and four horses at the door. "This man has returned," he said, "and my suspicions have done him less than justice." With that he spurred his horse, a signal which the trusty steed obeyed the more readily, as its progress was in the direction of the stable door. But when, dismounting, the Doctor hurried into his own house, it seemed to him, that the departure as well as the arrival of this distressed lady was destined to bring confusion to his peaceful dwelling. Several idlers had assembled about his door, and two or three had impudently thrust themselves forward almost into the passage, to listen to a confused altercation which was heard from within.

The Doctor hastened forward, the foremost of the intruders retreating in confusion on his approach, while he caught the tones of his wife's voice, raised to a pitch which he knew, by experience, boded no good; for Mrs. Gray, good-humoured and tractable in general, could sometimes perform the high part in a matrimonial duet. Having much more confidence in his wife's good intentions than her prudence, he lost no time in pushing into the parlour, to take the matter into his own hands. Here he found his helpmate at the head of the whole militia of the sick lady's apartment, that is, wet nurse, and sick nurse, and girl of all work, engaged in violent dispute with two strangers. The one was a dark-featured elderly man, with an eye of much sharpness and severity of expression, which now seemed partly quenched by a mixture of grief and mortification. The other, who appeared actively sustaining the dispute with Mrs. Gray, was a stout, bold-looking, hard-faced person, armed with pistols, of which he made rather an unnecessary and ostentatious display.

---

4   Strollers.

"Here is my husband, sir," said Mrs. Gray, in a tone of triumph, for she had the grace to believe the Doctor one of the greatest men living,—"Here is the Doctor—let us see what you will say now."

"Why just what I said before, ma'am," answered the man, "which is, that my warrant must be obeyed. It is regular, ma'am, regular."

So saying, he struck the forefinger of his right hand against a paper which he held towards Mrs. Gray with his left.

"Address yourself to me, if you please, sir," said the Doctor, seeing that he ought to lose no time in removing the cause into the proper court. "I am the master of this house, sir, and I wish to know the cause of this visit."

"My business is soon told," said the man. "I am a king's messenger, and this lady has treated me as if I was a baron-bailie's officer."

"That is not the question, sir," replied the Doctor. "If you are a king's messenger, where is your warrant, and what do you propose to do here?" At the same time he whispered the little wench to call Mr. Lawford, the town-clerk, to come thither as fast as he possibly could. The good-daughter of Peg Thomson started off with an activity worthy of her mother-in-law.

"There is my warrant," said the official, "and you may satisfy yourself."

"The shameless loon dare not tell the Doctor his errand," said Mrs. Gray exultingly.

"A bonny errand it is," said old Lucky Simson, "to carry away a lying-in woman as a gled⁵ would do a clocking-hen."

"A woman no a month delivered"—echoed the nurse Jamieson.

"Twenty-four days eight hours and seven minutes to a second," said Mrs. Gray.

The Doctor having looked over the warrant, which was regular, began to be afraid that the females of his family, in their zeal for defending the character of their sex, might be stirred up into some sudden fit of mutiny, and therefore commanded them to be silent.

"This," he said, "is a warrant for arresting the bodies of Richard Tresham, and of Zilia de Moncada on account of high treason. Sir, I have served his Majesty, and this is not a house in which traitors are harboured. I know nothing of any of these two persons, nor have I ever heard even their names."

"But the lady whom you have received into your family," said the messenger, "is Zilia de Moncada, and here stands her father, Matthias de Moncada, who will make oath to it."

"If this be true," said Mr. Gray, looking towards the alleged officer, "you have taken a singular duty on you. It is neither my habit to deny my own actions, nor to oppose the laws of the land. There is a lady in this house slowly recovering from confinement, having become under this roof the mother of a

---

5   Or Kite.

healthy child. If she be the person described in this warrant, and this gentle-man's daughter, I must surrender her to the laws of the country."

Here the Esculapian militia were once more in motion.

"Surrender, Dr. Gray! It's a shame to hear you speak, and you that lives by women and weans, abune your other means!" so exclaimed his fair better part.

"I wonder to hear the Doctor!" said the younger nurse; "there's no a wife in the town would believe it o' him."

"I aye thought the Doctor was a man till this moment," said Luckie Sim-son; "but I believe him now to be an auld wife, little baulder than mysell; and I dinna wonder that poor Mrs. Gray"—

"Hold your peace, you foolish woman," said the Doctor. "Do you think this business is not bad enough already, that you are making it worse with your senseless claver?[6]—Gentlemen, this is a very sad case. Here is a warrant for a high crime against a poor creature, who is little fit to be removed from one house to another, much more dragged to a prison. I tell you plainly, that I think the execution of this arrest may cause her death. It is your business, sir, if you be really her father, to consider what you can do to soften this matter, rather than drive it on."

"Better death than dishonour," replied the stern-looking old man, with a voice as harsh as his aspect; "and you, messenger," he continued, "look what you do, and execute the warrant at your peril."

"You hear," said the man, appealing to the Doctor himself, "I must have immediate access to the lady."

"In a lucky time," said Mr. Gray, "here comes the town-clerk.—You are very welcome, Mr. Lawford. Your opinion here is much wanted as a man of law, as well as of sense and humanity. I was never more glad to see you in all my life."

He then rapidly stated the case; and the messenger, understanding the new-comer to be a man of some authority, again exhibited his warrant.

"This is a very sufficient and valid warrant, Dr. Gray," replied the man of law. "Nevertheless, if you are disposed to make oath, that instant removal would be unfavourable to the lady's health, unquestionably she must remain here, suitably guarded."

"It is not so much the mere act of locomotion which I am afraid of," said the surgeon; "but I am free to depone, on soul and conscience, that the shame and fear of her father's anger, and the sense of the affront of such an arrest, with terror for its consequences, may occasion violent and dangerous illness—even death itself."

"The father must see the daughter, though they may have quarrelled," said Mr. Lawford; "the officer of justice must execute his warrant though it should

---

6 Tattling.

frighten the criminal to death; these evils are only contingent, not direct and immediate consequences. You must give up the lady, Mr. Gray, though your hesitation is very natural."

"At least, Mr. Lawford, I ought to be certain that the person in my house is the party they search for."

"Admit me to her apartment," replied the man whom the messenger termed Moncada.

The messenger, whom the presence of Lawford had made something more placid, began to become impudent once more. He hoped, he said, by means of his female prisoner, to acquire the information necessary to apprehend the more guilty person. If more delays were thrown in his way, that information might come too late, and he would make all who were accessary to such delay responsible for the consequences.

"And I," said Mr. Gray, "though I were to be brought to the gallows for it, protest, that this course may be the murder of my patient.—Can bail not be taken, Mr. Lawford?"

"Not in cases of high treason," said the official person; and then continued in a confidential tone, "Come, Mr. Gray, we all know you to be a person well affected to our Royal Sovereign King George and the Government; but you must not push this too far, lest you bring yourself into trouble, which every body in Middlemas would be sorry for. The forty-five has not been so far gone by, but we can remember enough of warrants of high treason—ay, and ladies of quality committed upon such charges. But they were all favourably dealt with—Lady Ogilvy, Lady Macintosh, Flora Macdonald, and all. No doubt this gentleman knows what he is doing, and has assurances of the young lady's safety—So you must jouk and let the jaw gae by, as we say."

"Follow me, then, gentleman," said Gideon, "and you shall see the young lady;" and then, his strong features working with emotion at anticipation of the distress which he was about to inflict, he led the way up the small staircase, and opening the door, said to Moncada, who had followed him, "This is your daughter's only place of refuge, in which I am, alas! too weak to be her protector. Enter, sir, if your conscience will permit you."

The stranger turned on him a scowl, into which it seemed as if he would willingly have thrown the power of the fabled basilisk. Then stepping proudly forward, he stalked into the room. He was followed by Lawford and Gray at a little distance. The messenger remained in the doorway. The unhappy young woman had heard the disturbance, and guessed the cause too truly. It is possible she might even have seen the strangers on their descent from the carriage. When they entered the room, she was on her knees, beside an easy chair, her face in a silk wrapper that was hung over it. The man called Moncada uttered a single word; by the accent it might have been something equivalent to *wretch*; but none knew its import.

The female gave a convulsive shudder, such as that by which a half-dying soldier is affected on receiving a second wound. But, without minding her emotion, Moncada seized her by the arm, and with little gentleness raised her to her feet, on which she seemed to stand only because she was supported by his strong grasp. He then pulled from her face the mask which she had hitherto worn. The poor creature still endeavoured to shroud her face, by covering it with her left hand, as the manner in which she was held prevented her from using the aid of the right. With little effort her father secured that hand also, which indeed was of itself far too little to serve the purpose of concealment, and showed her beautiful face, burning with blushes and covered with tears.

"You, Alcalde, and you, Surgeon," he said to Lawford and Gray, with a foreign action and accent, "this woman is my daughter, the same Zilia Moncada who is signal'd in that protocol. Make way, and let me carry her where her crimes may be atoned for."

"Are you that person's daughter?" said Lawford to the lady.

"She understands no English," said Gray; and addressing his patient in French, conjured her to let him know whether she was that man's daughter or not, assuring her of protection if the fact were otherwise. The answer was murmured faintly, but was too distinctly intelligible—"He was her father."

All farther title of interference seemed now ended. The messenger arrested his prisoner, and, with some delicacy, required the assistance of the females to get her conveyed to the carriage in waiting.

Gray again interfered.—"You will not," he said, "separate the mother and the infant?"

Zilia de Moncada heard the question, (which, being addressed to the father, Gray had inconsiderately uttered in French,) and it seemed as if it recalled to her recollection the existence of the helpless creature to which she had given birth, forgotten for a moment amongst the accumulated horrors of her father's presence. She uttered a shriek, expressing poignant grief, and turned her eyes on her father with the most intense supplication.

"To the parish with the bastard!"—said Moncada; while the helpless mother sunk lifeless into the arms of the females, who had now gathered round her.

"That will not pass, sir," said Gideon.—"If you are father to that lady, you must be grandfather to the helpless child; and you must settle in some manner for its future provision, or refer us to some responsible person."

Moncada looked towards Lawford, who expressed himself satisfied of the propriety of what Gray said.

"I object not to pay for whatever the wretched child may require," said he; "and if you, sir," addressing Gray, "choose to take charge of him, and breed him up, you shall have what will better your living."

The Doctor was about to refuse a charge so uncivilly offered; but after a moment's reflection, he replied, "I think so indifferently of the proceedings I have witnessed, and of those concerned in them, that if the mother desires that I should retain the charge of this child, I will not refuse to do so."

Moncada spoke to his daughter, who was just beginning to recover from her swoon, in the same language in which he had at first addressed her. The proposition which he made seemed highly acceptable, as she started from the arms of the females, and, advancing to Gray, seized his hand, kissed it, bathed it in her tears, and seemed reconciled, even in parting with her child, by the consideration, that the infant was to remain under his guardianship.

"Good, kind man," she said in her indifferent French, "you have saved both mother and child."

The father, meanwhile, with mercantile deliberation, placed in Mr. Lawford's hands notes and bills to the amount of a thousand pounds, which he stated was to be vested for the child's use, and advanced in such portions as his board and education might require. In the event of any correspondence on his account being necessary, as in case of death or the like, he directed that communication should be made to Signor Matthias Moncada, under cover to a certain banking house in London.

"But beware," he said to Gray, "how you trouble me about these concerns, unless in case of absolute necessity."

"You need not fear, sir," replied Gray; "I have seen nothing to-day which can induce me to desire a more intimate correspondence with you than may be indispensable."

While Lawford drew up a proper minute of this transaction, by which he himself and Gray were named trustees for the child, Mr. Gray attempted to restore to the lady the balance of the considerable sum of money which Tresham (if such was his real name) had formally deposited with him. With every species of gesture, by which hands, eyes, and even feet, could express rejection, as well as in her own broken French, she repelled the reimbursement, while she entreated that Gray would consider the money as his own property; and at the same time forced upon him a ring set with brilliants, which seemed of considerable value. The father then spoke to her a few stern words, which she heard with an air of mingled agony and submission.

"I have given her a few minutes to see and weep over the miserable being which has been the seal of her dishonour," said the stern father. "Let us retire and leave her alone.—You," to the messenger, "watch the door of the room on the outside."

Gray, Lawford, and Moncada, retired to the parlour accordingly, where they waited in silence, each busied with his own reflections, till, within the space of half an hour, they received information that the lady was ready to depart.

"It is well," replied Moncada; "I am glad she has yet sense enough left to submit to that which needs must be."

So saying, he ascended the stair, and returned leading down his daughter, now again masked and veiled. As she passed Gray, she uttered the words— "My child, my child!" in a tone of unutterable anguish; then entered the carriage, which was drawn up as close to the door of the doctor's house as the little enclosure would permit. The messenger, mounted on a led horse, and accompanied by a servant and assistant, followed the carriage, which drove rapidly off, taking the road which leads to Edinburgh. All who had witnessed this strange scene, now departed to make their conjectures, and some to count their gains; for money had been distributed among the females who had attended on the lady, with so much liberality, as considerably to reconcile them to the breach of the rights of womanhood inflicted by the precipitate removal of the patient.

CHAPTER 2

The last cloud of dust which the wheels of the carriage had raised was dissipated, when dinner, which claims a share of human thoughts even in the midst of the most marvellous and affecting incidents, recurred to those of Mrs. Gray.

"Indeed, Doctor, you will stand glowering out of the window till some other patient calls for you, and then have to set off without your dinner;—and I hope Mr. Lawford will take pot-luck with us, for it is just his own hour; and indeed we had something rather better than ordinary for this poor lady—lamb and spinage, and a veal Florentine."

The surgeon started as from a dream, and joined in his wife's hospitable request, to which Lawford willingly assented.

We will suppose the meal finished, a bottle of old and generous Antigua upon the table, and a modest little punch-bowl, judiciously replenished for the accommodation of the Doctor and his guest. Their conversation naturally turned on the strange scene which they had witnessed, and the Townclerk took considerable merit for his presence of mind.

"I am thinking, Doctor," said he, "you might have brewed a bitter browst to yourself if I had not come in as I did."

"Troth, and it might very well so be," answered Gray; "for, to tell you the truth, when I saw yonder fellow vapouring with his pistols among the woman-folk in my own house, the old Cameronian spirit began to rise in me, and little thing would have made me cleek to the poker."

"Hoot, hoot! that would never have done. Na, na," said the man of law, "this was a case where a little prudence was worth all the pistols and pokers in the world."

"And that was just what I thought when I sent to you, Clerk Lawford," said the Doctor.

"A wiser man he could not have called on to a difficult case," added Mrs. Gray, as she sat with her work at a little distance from the table.

"Thanks t'ye, and here's t'ye, my good neighbour," answered the scribe; "will you not let me help you to another glass of punch, Mrs. Gray?" This being declined, he proceeded. "I am jalousing that the messenger and his warrant were just brought in to prevent any opposition. Ye saw how quietly he behaved after I had laid down the law—I'll never believe the lady is in any risk from him. But the father is a dour chield; depend upon it, he has bred up the young filly on the curb-rein, and that has made the poor thing start off the course. I should not be surprised that he took her abroad, and shut her up in a convent."

"Hardly," replied Doctor Gray, "if it be true, as I suspect, that both the father and daughter are of the Jewish persuasion."

"A Jew!" said Mrs. Gray; "and have I been taking a' this fyke about a Jew?—I thought she seemed to gie a scunner at the eggs and bacon that Nurse Simson spoke about to her. But I thought Jews had aye had lang beards, and yon man's face is just like one of our ain folk's—I have seen the Doctor with a langer beard himsell, when he has not had leisure to shave."

"That might have been Mr. Moncada's case," said Lawford, "for he seemed to have had a hard journey. But the Jews are often very respectable people, Mrs. Gray—they have no territorial property, because the law is against them there, but they have a good hank in the money market—plenty of stock in the funds, Mrs. Gray, and, indeed, I think this poor young woman is better with her ain father, though he be a Jew and a dour chield into the bargain, than she would have been with the loon that wranged her, who is, by your account, Dr. Gray, baith a papist and a rebel. The Jews are well attached to government; they hate the Pope, the Devil, and the Pretender, as much as any honest man among ourselves."

"I cannot admire either of the gentlemen," said Gideon. "But it is but fair to say, that I saw Mr. Moncada when he was highly incensed, and to all appearance not without reason. Now, this other man Tresham, if that be his name, was haughty to me, and I think something careless of the poor young woman, just at the time when he owed her most kindness, and me some thankfulness. I am, therefore, of your opinion, Clerk Lawford, that the Christian is the worse bargain of the two."

"And you think of taking care of this wean yourself, Doctor? That is what I call the good Samaritan."

"At cheap cost. Clerk; the child, if it lives, has enough to bring it up decently, and set it out in life, and I can teach it an honourable and useful profession. It will be rather an amusement than a trouble to me, and I want to make some remarks on the childish diseases, which, with God's blessing, the child must come through under my charge; and since Heaven has sent us no children"—

"Hoot, hoot!" said the Town-Clerk, "you are in ower great hurry now—you have na been sae lang married yet.—Mrs. Gray, dinna let my daffing chase you away—we will be for a dish of tea believe, for the Doctor and I are nae glass-breakers."

Four years after this conversation took place, the event happened, at the possibility of which the Town-Clerk had hinted; and Mrs. Gray presented her husband with an infant daughter. But good and evil are strangely mingled in this sublunary world. The fulfilment of his anxious longing for posterity was attended with the loss of his simple and kind-hearted wife; one of the most heavy blows which fate could inflict on poor Gideon, and, his house was made desolate even by the event which had promised for months before to add new comforts to its humble roof. Gray felt the shock as men of sense and firmness feel a decided blow, from the effects of which they never hope again fully to raise themselves. He discharged the duties of his profession with the same punctuality as ever, was easy, and even to appearance, cheerful in his intercourse with society; but the sunshine of existence was gone. Every morning he missed the affectionate charges which recommended to him to pay attention to his own health while he was labouring to restore that blessing to his patients. Every evening, as he returned from his weary round, it was without the consciousness of a kind and affectionate reception from one eager to tell, and interested to hear, all the little events of the day. His whistle, which used to arise clear and strong so soon as Middlemas steeple was in view, was now for ever silenced, and the rider's head drooped, while the tired horse, lacking the stimulus of his master's hand and voice, seemed to shuffle along as if it experienced a share of his despondency. There were times when he was so much dejected as to be unable to endure even the presence of his little Menie, in whose infant countenance he could trace the lineaments of the mother, of whose loss she had been the innocent and unconscious cause. "Had it not been for this poor child"—he would think; but, instantly aware that the sentiment was sinful, he would snatch the infant to his breast, and load it with caresses—then hastily desire it to be removed from the parlour.

The Mahometans have a fanciful idea, that the true believer, in his passage to Paradise, is under the necessity of passing barefooted over a bridge composed of red-hot iron. But on this occasion, all the pieces of paper which the Moslem has preserved during his life, lest some holy thing being written upon them might be profaned, arrange themselves between his feet and the burning metal, and so save him from injury. In the same manner, the effects of kind and benevolent actions are sometimes found, even in this world, to assuage the pangs of subsequent afflictions.

Thus, the greatest consolation which poor Gideon could find after his heavy deprivation, was in the frolic fondness of Richard Middlemas, the child who was in so singular a manner thrown upon his charge. Even at this early age he was eminently handsome. When silent or out of humour, his dark eyes and striking countenance presented some recollections of the stern character imprinted on the features of his supposed father; but when he was gay and happy, which was much more frequently the case, these clouds were exchanged for the most frolicsome, mirthful expression, that ever dwelt on the laughing and thoughtless aspect of a child. He seemed to have a tact beyond his years in discovering and conforming to the peculiarities of human character. His nurse, one prime object of Richard's observance, was Nurse Jamieson, or, as she was more commonly called for brevity, and *par excellence*, Nurse. This was the person who had brought him up from infancy. She had lost her own child, and soon after her husband, and being thus a lone woman, had, as used to be common in Scotland, remained a member of Dr. Gray's family. After the death of his wife, she gradually obtained the principal superintendence of the whole household; and being an honest and capable manager, was a person of very great importance in the family.

She was bold in her temper, violent in her feelings, and, as often happens with those in her condition, was as much attached to Richard Middlemas, whom she had once nursed at her bosom, as if he had been her own son. This affection the child repaid by all the tender attentions of which his age was capable.

Little Dick was also distinguished by the fondest and kindest attachment to his guardian and benefactor Dr. Gray. He was officious in the right time and place, quiet as a lamb when his patron seemed inclined to study or to muse, active and assiduous to assist or divert him whenever it seemed to be wished, and, in choosing his opportunities, he seemed to display an address far beyond his childish years.

As time passed on, this pleasing character seemed to be still more refined. In everything like exercise or amusement, he was the pride and the leader of the boys of the place, over the most of whom his strength and activity gave him a decided superiority. At school his abilities were less distinguished, yet he was a favourite with the master, a sensible and useful teacher.

"Richard is not swift," he used to say to his patron, Dr. Gray, "but then he is sure; and it is impossible not to be pleased with a child who is so very desirous to give satisfaction."

Young Middlemas's grateful affection to his patron seemed to increase with the expanding of his faculties, and found a natural and pleasing mode of displaying itself in his attentions to little Menie [7] Gray. Her slightest hint was

---

7 Marion.

Richard's law, and it was in vain that he was summoned forth by a hundred shrill voices to take the lead in hye-spye, or at foot-ball, if it was little Menie's pleasure that he should remain within, and build card-houses for her amusement. At other times he would take the charge of the little damsel entirely under his own care, and be seen wandering with her on the borough common, collecting wild flowers, or knitting caps made of bulrushes. Menie was attached to Dick Middlemas, in proportion to his affectionate assiduities; and the father saw with pleasure every new mark of attention to his child on the part of his protege.

During the time that Richard was silently advancing from a beautiful child into a fine boy, and approaching from a fine boy to the time when he must be termed a handsome youth, Mr. Gray wrote twice a-year with much regularity to Mr. Moncada, through the channel that gentleman had pointed out. The benevolent man thought, that if the wealthy grandfather could only see his relative, of whom any family might be proud, he would be unable to persevere in his resolution of treating as an outcast one so nearly connected with him in blood, and so interesting in person and disposition. He thought it his duty, therefore, to keep open the slender and oblique communication with the boy's maternal grandfather, as that which might, at some future period, lead to a closer connexion. Yet the correspondence could not, in other respects, be agreeable to a man of spirit like Mr. Gray. His own letters were as short as possible, merely rendering an account of his ward's expenses, including a moderate board to himself, attested by Mr. Lawford, his co-trustee; and intimating Richard's state of health, and his progress in education, with a few words of brief but warm eulogy upon his goodness of head and heart. But the answers he received were still shorter. "Mr. Moncada," such was their usual tenor, "acknowledges Mr. Gray's letter of such a date, notices the contents, and requests Mr. Gray to persist in the plan which he has hitherto prosecuted on the subject of their correspondence." On occasions where extraordinary expenses seemed likely to be incurred, the remittances were made with readiness.

That day fortnight after Mrs. Gray's death, fifty pounds were received, with a note, intimating that it was designed to put the child R. M. into proper mourning. The writer had added two or three words, desiring that the surplus should be at Mr. Gray's disposal, to meet the additional expenses of this period of calamity; but Mr. Moncada had left the phrase unfinished, apparently in despair of turning it suitably into English. Gideon, without farther investigation, quietly added the sum to the account of his ward's little fortune, contrary to the opinion of Mr. Lawford,—who, aware that he was rather a loser than a gainer by the boy's residence in his house, was desirous that his friend should not omit an opportunity of recovering some part of his expenses on that score. But Gray was proof against all remonstrances.

43

As the boy advanced towards his fourteenth year, Dr. Gray wrote a more elaborate account of his ward's character, acquirements, and capacity. He added that he did this for the purpose of enabling Mr. Moncada to judge how the young man's future education should be directed. Richard, he observed, was arrived at the point where education, losing its original and general character, branches off into different paths of knowledge, suitable to particular professions, and when it was therefore become necessary to determine which of them it was his pleasure that young Richard should be trained for; and he would, on his part, do all he could to carry Mr. Moncada's wishes into execution, since the amiable qualities of the boy made him as dear to him, though but a guardian, as he could have been to his own father.

The answer, which arrived in the course of a week or ten days, was fuller than usual, and written in the first person.—"Mr. Gray," such was the tenor, "our meeting has been under such circumstances as could not make us favourably known to each other at the time. But I have the advantage of you, since, knowing your motives for entertaining an indifferent opinion of me, I could respect them, and you at the same time; whereas you, unable to comprehend the motives—I say, you, being unacquainted with the infamous treatment I had received, could not understand the reasons that I have for acting as I have done. Deprived, sir, by the act of a villain, of my child, and she despoiled of honour, I cannot bring myself to think of beholding the creature, however innocent, whose look must always remind me of hatred and of shame. Keep the poor child by you—educate him to your own profession, but take heed that he looks no higher than to fill such a situation in life as you yourself worthily occupy, or some other line of like importance. For the condition of a farmer, a country lawyer, a medical practitioner, or some such retired course of life, the means of outfit and education shall be amply supplied. But I must warn him and you, that any attempt to intrude himself on me further than I may especially permit, will be attended with the total forfeiture of my favour and protection. So, having made known my mind to you, I expect you will act accordingly."

The receipt of this letter determined Gideon to have some explanation with the boy himself, in order to learn if he had any choice among the professions thus opened to him; convinced at the same time, from his docility of temper, that he would refer the selection to his (Dr. Gray's) better judgment.

He had previously, however, the unpleasing task of acquainting Richard Middlemas with the mysterious circumstances attending his birth, of which he presumed him to be entirely ignorant, simply because he himself had never communicated them, but had let the boy consider himself as the orphan child of a distant relation. But though the Doctor himself was silent, he might have remembered that Nurse Jamieson had the handsome enjoyment of her tongue, and was disposed to use it liberally.

From a very early period, Nurse Jamieson, amongst the variety of legendary lore which she instilled into her foster-son, had not forgotten what she called the awful season of his coming into the world—the personable appearance of his father, a grand gentleman, who looked as if the whole world lay at his feet—the beauty of his mother, and the terrible blackness of the mask which she wore, her een that glanced like diamonds, and the diamonds she wore on her fingers, that could be compared to nothing but her own een, the fairness of her skin, and the colour of her silk rokelay, with much proper stuff to the same purpose. Then she expatiated on the arrival of his grandfather, and the awful man, armed with pistol, dirk, and claymore, (the last weapons existed only in Nurse's imagination,) the very Ogre of a fairy tale—then all the circumstances of the carrying off his mother, while bank-notes were flying about the house like screeds of brown paper, and gold guineas were as plenty as chuckie-stanes. All this, partly to please and interest the boy, partly to indulge her own talent for amplification, Nurse told with so many additional circumstances, and gratuitous commentaries, that the real transaction, mysterious and odd as it certainly was sunk into tameness before the Nurse's edition, like humble prose contrasted with the boldest nights of poetry.

To hear all this did Richard seriously incline, and still more was he interested with the idea of his valiant father coming for him unexpectedly at the head of a gallant regiment, with music playing and colours flying, and carrying his son away on the most beautiful pony eyes ever beheld; Or his mother, bright as the day, might suddenly appear in her coach-and-six, to reclaim her beloved child; or his repentant grandfather, with his pockets stuffed out with banknotes, would come to atone for his past cruelty, by heaping his neglected grandchild with unexpected wealth. Sure was Nurse Jamieson, "that it wanted but a blink of her bairn's bonny ee to turn their hearts, as Scripture sayeth; and as strange things had been, as they should come a'thegither to the town at the same time, and make such a day as had never been seen in Middlemas; and then her bairn would never be called by that Lowland name of Middlemas any more, which sounded as if it had been gathered out of the town gutter; but would be called Galatian,[8] or Sir William Wallace, or Robin Hood, or after some other of the great princes named in story-books."

Nurse Jamieson's history of the past, and prospects of the future, were too flattering not to excite the most ambitious visions in the mind of a boy, who naturally felt a strong desire of rising in the world, and was conscious of possessing the powers necessary to his advancement. The incidents of his birth resembled those he found commemorated in the tales which he read or listened to; and there seemed no reason why his own adventures should not

---

8   Galatian is a name of a person famous in Christmas gambols.

have a termination corresponding to those of such veracious histories. In a word, while good Doctor Gray imagined that his pupil was dwelling in utter ignorance of his origin, Richard was meditating upon nothing else than the time and means by which he anticipated his being extricated from the obscurity of his present condition, and enabled to assume the rank, to which, in his own opinion, he was entitled by birth.

So stood the feelings of the young man, when, one day after dinner, the Doctor snuffing the candle, and taking from his pouch the great leathern pocketbook in which he deposited particular papers, with a small supply of the most necessary and active medicines, he took from it Mr. Moncada's letter, and requested Richard Middlemas's serious attention, while he told him some circumstances concerning himself, which it greatly imported him to know. Richard's dark eyes flashed fire—the blood flushed his broad and well-formed forehead—the hour of explanation was at length come. He listened to the narrative of Gideon Gray, which, the reader may believe, being altogether divested of the gilding which Nurse Jamieson's imagination had bestowed upon it, and reduced to what mercantile men termed the *needful*, exhibited little more than the tale of a child of shame, deserted by its father and mother, and brought up on the reluctant charity of a more distant relation, who regarded him as the living though unconscious evidence of the disgrace of his family, and would more willingly have paid for the expenses of his funeral, than that of the food which was grudgingly provided for him. "Temple and tower," a hundred flattering edifices of Richard's childish imagination, went to the ground at once, and the pain which attended their demolition was rendered the more acute, by a sense of shame that he should have nursed such reveries. He remained while Gideon continued his explanation, in a dejected posture, his eyes fixed on the ground, and the veins of his forehead swoln with contending passions.

"And now, my dear Richard," said the good surgeon, "you must think what you can do for yourself, since your grandfather leaves you the choice of three honourable professions, by any of which, well and wisely prosecuted, you may become independent if not wealthy, and respectable if not great. You will naturally desire a little time for consideration."

"Not a minute," said the boy, raising his head, and looking boldly at his guardian. "I am a free-born Englishman, and will return to England if I think fit."

"A free-born fool you are,"—said Gray; "you were born, as I think, and no one can know better than I do, in the blue room of Stevenlaw's Land, in the Town-head of Middlemas, if you call that being a free-born Englishman."

"But Tom Hillary,"—this was an apprentice of Clerk Lawford, who had of late been a great friend and adviser of young Middlemas—"Tom Hillary says that I am a free-born Englishman, notwithstanding, in right of my parents."

"Pooh, child! what do we know of your parents?—But what has your being an Englishman to do with the present question?"

"Oh, Doctor!" answered the boy bitterly, "you know we from the south side of Tweed cannot scramble so hard as you do. The Scots are too moral, and too prudent, and too robust, for a poor pudding-eater to live amongst them, whether as a parson, or as a lawyer, or as a doctor—with your pardon, sir."

"Upon my life, Dick," said Gray, "this Tom Hillary will turn your brain. What is the meaning of all this trash?"

"Tom Hillary says that the parson lives by the sins of the people, the lawyer by their distresses, and the doctor by their diseases—always asking your pardon, sir."

"Tom Hillary," replied the Doctor, "should be drummed out of the borough. A whipper-snapper of an attorney's apprentice, run away from Newcastle! If I hear him talking so, I'll teach him to speak with more reverence of the learned professions. Let me hear no more of Tom Hillary whom you have seen far too much of lately. Think a little, like a lad of sense, and tell me what answer I am to give to Mr. Moncada."

"Tell him," said the boy, the tone of affected sarcasm laid aside, and that of injured pride substituted in its room, "Tell him that my soul revolts at the obscure lot he recommends to me. I am determined to enter my father's profession, the army, unless my grandfather chooses to receive me into his house, and place me in his own line of business."

"Yes, and make you his partner, I suppose, and acknowledge you for his heir?" said Dr. Gray; "a thing extremely likely to happen, no doubt, considering the way in which he has brought you up all along, and the terms in which he now writes concerning you."

"Then, sir, there is one thing which I can demand of you," replied the boy. "There is a large sum of money in your hands belonging to me; and since it is consigned to you for my use, I demand you should make the necessary advances to procure a commission in the army—account to me for the balance—and so, with thanks for past favours, I will give you no trouble in future."

"Young man," said the Doctor, gravely, "I am very sorry to see that your usual prudence and good humour are not proof against the disappointment of some idle expectations which you had not the slightest reason to entertain. It is very true that there is a sum, which, in spite of various expenses, may still approach to a thousand pounds or better, which remains in my hands for your behoof. But I am bound to dispose of it according to the will of the donor; and at any rate, you are not entitled to call for it until you come to years of discretion; a period from which you are six years distant, according to law, and which, in one sense, you will never reach at all, unless you alter your present unreasonable crotchets. But come, Dick, this is the first time I have seen you in so absurd a humour, and you have many things, I own, in your situation to apologize for impatience even greater than you have displayed. But you should not turn your resentment on me, that am no way in fault. You should remember that I was your earliest and only friend, and took charge of you when every other person forsook you."

"I do not thank you for it," said Richard, giving way to a burst of uncontrolled passion. "You might have done better for me had you pleased."

"And in what manner, you ungrateful boy?" said Gray, whose composure was a little ruffled.

"You might have flung me under the wheels of their carriages as they drove off, and have let them trample on the body of their child, as they have done on his feelings."

So saying, he rushed out of the room, and shut the door behind him with great violence, leaving his guardian astonished at his sudden and violent change of temper and manner.

"What the deuce can have possessed him? Ah, well. High-spirited, and disappointed in some follies which that Tom Hillary has put into his head. But his is a case for anodynes, and shall be treated accordingly."

While the Doctor formed this good-natured resolution, young Middlemas rushed to Nurse Jamieson's apartment, where poor Menie, to whom his presence always gave holyday feelings, hastened to exhibit, for his admiration, a new doll, of which she had made the acquisition. No one, generally, was more interested in Menie's amusements than Richard; but at present, Richard, like his celebrated namesake, was not i'the vein. He threw off the little damsel so carelessly, almost so rudely, that the doll flew out of Menie's hand, fell on the hearth-stone, and broke its waxen face. The rudeness drew from Nurse Jamieson a rebuke, even although the culprit was her darling.

"Hout awa', Richard—that wasna like yoursell, to guide Miss Menie that gate.—Haud your tongue, Miss Menie, and I'll soon mend the baby's face."

But if Menie cried, she did not cry for the doll; and while the tears flowed silently down her cheeks, she sat looking at Dick Middlemas with a childish face of fear, sorrow, and wonder. Nurse Jamieson was soon diverted from her attention to Menie Gray's distresses, especially as she did not weep aloud, and her attention became fixed on the altered countenance, red eyes, and swoln features of her darling foster-child. She instantly commenced an investigation into the cause of his distress, after the usual inquisitorial manner of matrons of her class. "What is the matter wi' my bairn?" and "Wha has been vexing my bairn?" with similar questions, at last extorted this reply:

"I am not your bairn—I am no one's bairn—no one's son. I am an outcast from my family, and belong to no one. Dr. Gray has told me so himself."

"And did he cast up to my bairn that he was a bastard?—troth he was na blate—my certie, your father was a better man than ever stood on the

Doctor's shanks—a handsome grand gentleman, with an ee like a gled's, and a step like a Highland piper."

Nurse Jamieson had got on a favourite topic, and would have expatiated long enough, for she was a professed admirer of masculine beauty, but there was something which displeased the boy in her last simile; so he cut the conversation short, by asking whether she knew exactly how much money his grandfather had left with Dr. Gray for his maintenance. "She could not say—didna ken—an awfu' sum it was to pass out of ae man's hand—She was sure it wasna less than ae hundred pounds, and it might weel be twa." In short, she knew nothing about the matter; "but she was sure Dr. Gray would count to him to the last farthing; for everybody kend that he was a just man where siller was concerned. However, if her bairn wanted to ken mair about it, to be sure the Town-clerk could tell him all about it."

Richard Middlemas arose and left the apartment, without saying more. He went immediately to visit the old Town-clerk, to whom he had made himself acceptable, as, indeed, he had done to most of the dignitaries about the burgh. He introduced the conversation by the proposal which had been made to him for choosing a profession, and, after speaking of the mysterious circumstances of his birth, and the doubtful prospects which lay before him, he easily led the Town-clerk into conversation as to the amount of the funds, and heard the exact state of the money in his guardian's hands, which corresponded with the information he had already received. He next sounded the worthy scribe on the possibility of his going into the army; but received a second confirmation of the intelligence Mr. Gray had given him; being informed that no part of the money could be placed at his disposal till he was of age; and then not without the especial consent of both his guardians, and particularly that of his master. He therefore took leave of the Town-clerk, who, much approving the cautious manner in which he spoke, and his prudent selection of an adviser at this important crisis of his life, intimated to him, that should he choose the law, he would himself receive him into his office, upon a very moderate apprentice-fee, and would part with Tom Hillary to make room for him, as the lad was "rather pragmatical, and plagued him with speaking about his English practice, which they had nothing to do with on this side of the Border—the Lord be thanked!"

Middlemas thanked him for his kindness, and promised to consider his kind offer, in case he should determine upon following the profession of the law.

From Tom Hillary's master, Richard went to Tom Hillary himself, who chanced then to be in the office. He was a lad about twenty, as smart as small, but distinguished for the accuracy with which he dressed his hair, and the splendour of a laced hat and embroidered waistcoat, with which he graced the church of Middlemas on Sundays. Tom Hillary had been bred an attorney's clerk in Newcastle-upon-Tyne, but, for some reason or other, had found it more convenient of late years to reside in Scotland, and was recommended to the Town-clerk of Middlemas, by the accuracy and beauty with which he transcribed the records of the burgh. It is not improbable that the reports concerning the singular circumstances of Richard Middlemas's birth, and the knowledge that he was actually possessed of a considerable sum of money, induced Hillary, though so much his senior, to admit the lad to his company, and enrich his youthful mind with some branches of information, which in that retired corner, his pupil might otherwise have been some time in attaining. Amongst these were certain games at cards and dice, in which the pupil paid, as was reasonable, the price of initiation by his losses to his instructor. After a long walk with this youngster, whose advice, like the unwise son of the wisest of men, he probably valued more than that of his more aged counsellors, Richard Middlemas returned to his lodgings in Stevenlaw's Land, and went to bed sad and supperless.

The next morning Richard arose with the sun, and his night's rest appeared to have had its frequent effect, in cooling the passions and correcting the understanding. Little Menie was the first person to whom he made the *amende honorable;* and a much smaller propitiation than the new doll with which he presented her would have been accepted as an atonement for a much greater offence. Menie was one of those pure spirits, to whom a state of unkindness, if the estranged person has been a friend, is a state of pain, and the slightest advance of her friend and protector was sufficient to regain all her childish confidence and affection.

The father did not prove more inexorable than Menie had done. Mr. Gray, indeed, thought he had good reason to look cold upon Richard at their next meeting, being not a little hurt at the ungrateful treatment which he had received on the preceding evening. But Middlemas disarmed him at once, by frankly pleading that he had suffered his mind to be carried away by the supposed rank and importance of his parents, into an idle conviction that he was one day to share them. The letter of his grandfather, which condemned him to banishment and obscurity for life, was, he acknowledged, a very severe blow; and it was with deep sorrow that he reflected, that the irritation of his disappointment had led him to express himself in a manner far short of the respect and reverence of one who owed Mr. Gray the duty and affection of a son, and ought to refer to his decision every action of his life. Gideon, propitiated by an admission so candid, and made with so much humility, readily dismissed his resentment, and kindly enquired of Richard, whether he had bestowed any reflection upon the choice of profession which had been subjected to him; offering, at the same time, to allow him all reasonable time to make up his mind.

On this subject. Richard Middlemas answered with the same prompt-titude and candour.—"He had," he said, "in order to forming his opinion more safely, consulted with his friend, the Town-clerk." The Doctor nodded approbation. "Mr. Lawford had, indeed, been most friendly, and had even offered to take him into his own office. But if his father and benefactor would permit him to study, under his instructions, the noble art in which he himself enjoyed such a deserved reputation, the mere hope that he might by-and-by be of some use to Mr. Gray in his business, would greatly overbalance every other consideration. Such a course of education, and such a use of professional knowledge when he had acquired it, would be a greater spur to his industry than the prospect even of becoming Town-clerk of Middlemas in his proper person."

As the young man expressed it to be his firm and unalterable choice, to study medicine under his guardian, and to remain a member of his family, Dr. Gray informed Mr. Moncada of the lad's determination; who, to testify his approbation, remitted to the Doctor the sum of L100 as apprentice fee, a sum nearly three times as much as Gray's modesty had hinted at as necessary.

Shortly after, when Dr. Gray and the Town-clerk met at the small club of the burgh, their joint theme was the sense and steadiness of Richard Middlemas.

"Indeed," said the Town-clerk, "he is such a friendly and disinterested boy, that I could not get him to accept a place in my office, for fear he should be thought to be pushing himself forward at the expense of Tam Hillary."

"And, indeed, Clerk," said Gray, "I have sometimes been afraid that he kept too much company with that Tam Hillary of yours; but twenty Tam Hillarys would not corrupt Dick Middlemas."

CHAPTER 3

Dick was come to high renown
    Since he commenced physician;
Tom was held by all the town
    The better politician.

TOM AND DICK.

At the same period when Dr. Gray took under his charge his youthful lodger Richard Middlemas, he received proposals from the friends of one Adam Hartley, to receive him also as an apprentice. The lad was the son of a respectable farmer on the English side of the Border, who educating his eldest son to his own occupation, desired to make his second a medical man, in order to avail himself of the friendship of a great man, his landlord, who had offered to assist his views in life, and represented a doctor or surgeon as the sort of person to whose advantage his interest could be most readily applied. Middlemas and Hartley were therefore associated in their studies. In winter they were boarded in Edinburgh, for attending the medical classes which were necessary for taking their degree. Three or four years thus passed on, and, from being mere boys, the two medical aspirants shot up into young men, who, being both very good-looking, well dressed, well bred, and having money in their pockets, became personages of some importance in the little town of Middlemas, where there was scarce any thing that could be termed an aristocracy, and in which beaux were scarce and belles were plenty.

Each of the two had his especial partizans; for though the young men themselves lived in tolerable harmony together, yet, as usual in such cases, no one could approve of one of them, without at the same time comparing him with, and asserting his superiority over his companion.

Both were gay, fond of dancing, and sedulous attendants on the *practeezings*, as he called them, of Mr. McFittoch, a dancing master, who, itinerant during the summer, became stationary in the winter season, and afforded the youth of Middlemas the benefit of his instructions at the rate of twenty lessons for five shillings sterling. On these occasions, each of Dr. Gray's pupils had his appropriate praise. Hartley danced with most spirit—Middlemas with a better grace. Mr. McFittoch would have turned out Richard against the country-side in the minuet, and wagered the thing dearest to him in the world, (and that was his kit,) upon his assured superiority; but he admitted Hartley was superior to him in hornpipes, jigs, strathspeys, and reels.

In dress, Hartley was most expensive, perhaps because his father afforded him better means of being so; but his clothes were neither so tasteful when new, nor so well preserved when they began to grow old, as those of Richard Middlemas. Adam Hartley was sometimes fine, at other times rather slovenly, and on the former occasions looked rather too conscious of his splendour. His chum was at all times regularly neat and well dressed; while at the same time he had an air of good-breeding, which made him appear always at ease; so that his dress, whatever it was, seemed to be just what he ought to have worn at the time.

In their persons there was a still more strongly marked distinction. Adam Hartley was full middle size, stout, and well limbed; and an open English countenance, of the genuine Saxon mould, showed itself among chestnut locks, until the hair-dresser destroyed them. He loved the rough exercises of wrestling, boxing, leaping, and quarterstaff, and frequented, when he could obtain leisure, the bull-baitings and foot-ball matches, by which the burgh was sometimes enlivened.

Richard, on the contrary, was dark, like his father and mother, with high features, beautifully formed, but exhibiting something of a foreign character; and his person was tall and slim, though muscular and active. His address and manners must have been natural to him, for they were, in elegance and ease, far beyond any example which he could have found in his native burgh. He learned the use of the small-sword while in Edinburgh, and took lessons from a performer at the theatre, with the purpose of refining his mode of speaking. He became also an amateur of the drama, regularly attending the playhouse, and assuming the tone of a critic in that and other lighter departments of literature. To fill up the contrast, so far as taste was concerned, Richard was a dexterous and successful angler—Adam, a bold and unerring shot. Their efforts to surpass each other in supplying Dr. Gray's table, rendered his housekeeping much preferable to what it had been on former occasions; and, besides, small presents of fish and game are always agreeable amongst the inhabitants of a country town, and contributed to increase the popularity of the young sportsmen.

While the burgh was divided, for lack of better subject of disputation, concerning the comparative merits of Dr. Gray's two apprentices, he himself was sometimes chosen the referee. But in this, as on other matters, the Doctor was cautious. He said the lads were both good lads, and would be useful men in the profession, if their heads were not carried with the notice which the foolish people of the burgh took of them, and the parties of pleasure that were so often taking them away from their business. No doubt it was natural for him to feel more confidence in Hartley, who came of ken'd folk, and was very near as good as a born Scotsman. But if he did feel such a partiality, he blamed himself for it, since the stranger child, so oddly cast upon his hands, had peculiar good right to such patronage and affection as he had to bestow; and truly the young man himself seemed so grateful, that it was impossible for him to hint the slightest wish, that Dick Middlemas did not hasten to execute.

There were persons in the burgh of Middlemas who were indiscreet enough to suppose that Miss Menie must be a better judge than any other person of the comparative merits of these accomplished personages, respecting which the public opinion was generally divided. No one even of her greatest intimates ventured to put the question to her in precise terms; but her conduct was narrowly observed, and the critics remarked, that to Adam Hartley her attentions were given more freely and frankly. She laughed with him, chatted with him, and danced with him; while to Dick Middlemas her conduct was more shy and distant. The premises seemed certain, but the public were divided in the conclusions which were to be drawn from them.

It was not possible for the young men to be the subject of such discussions without being sensible that they existed; and thus, contrasted together by the little society in which they moved, they must have been made of better than ordinary clay, if they had not themselves entered by degrees into the spirit of the controversy, and considered themselves as rivals for public applause.

Nor is it to be forgotten, that Menie Gray was by this time shot up into one of the prettiest young women, not of Middlemas only, but of the whole county, in which the little burgh is situated. This, indeed, had been settled by evidence, which could not be esteemed short of decisive. At the time of the races, there were usually assembled in the burgh some company of the higher classes from the country around, and many of the sober burghers mended their incomes, by letting their apartments, or taking in lodgers of quality for the busy week. All the rural thanes and thanesses attended on these occasions; and such was the number of cocked hats and silken trains, that the little town seemed for a time totally to have changed its inhabitants. On this occasion persons of a certain quality only were permitted to attend upon the nightly balls which were given in the old Town-house, and the line of distinction excluded Mr. Gray's family.

The aristocracy, however, used their privileges with some feelings of deference to the native beaux and belles of the burgh, who were thus doomed to hear the fiddles nightly, without being permitted to dance to them. One evening in the race-week, termed the Hunter's ball, was dedicated to general amusement, and liberated from the usual restrictions of etiquette. On this occasion all the respectable families in the town were invited to share the amusement of the evening, and to wonder at the finery, and be grateful for the condescension, of their betters. This was especially the case with the females, for the number of invitations to the gentlemen of the town was much more limited. Now, at this general muster, the beauty of Miss Gray's face and person had placed her, in the opinion of all competent judges, decidedly at the head of all the belles present, saving those with whom, according to the ideas of the place, it would hardly have been decent to compare her.

The Laird of the ancient and distinguished house of Louponheight did not hesitate to engage her hand during the greater part of the evening; and his mother, renowned for her stern assertion of the distinctions of rank, placed the little plebeian beside her at supper, and was heard to say, that the surgeon's daughter behaved very prettily indeed, and seemed to know perfectly well where and what she was. As for the young Laird himself, he capered so high, and laughed so uproariously, as to give rise to a rumour, that he was minded to "shoot madly from his sphere," and to convert the village Doctor's daughter into a lady of his own ancient name.

During this memorable evening, Middlemas and Hartley, who had found room in the music gallery, witnessed the scene, and, as it would seem, with very different feelings. Hartley was evidently annoyed by the excess of attention which the gallant Laird of Louponheight, stimulated by the influence of a couple of bottles of claret, and by the presence of a partner who danced remarkably well, paid to Miss Menie Gray. He saw from his lofty stand all the dumb show of gallantry, with the comfortable feelings of a famishing creature looking upon a feast which he is not permitted to share, and regarded every extraordinary frisk of the jovial Laird, as the same might have been looked upon by a gouty person, who apprehended that the dignitary was about to descend on his toes. At length, unable to restrain his emotion, he left the gallery and returned no more.

Far different was the demeanour of Middlemas. He seemed gratified and elevated by the attention which was generally paid to Miss Gray, and by the admiration she excited. On the valiant Laird of Louponheight he looked with indescribable contempt, and amused himself with pointing out to the burgh dancing-master, who acted *pro tempore* as one of the band, the frolicsome bounds and pirouettes, in which that worthy displayed a great deal more of vigour than of grace.

"But ye shouldna laugh sae loud, Master Dick," said the master of capers; "he hasna had the advantage of a real gracefu' teacher, as ye have had; and troth, if he listed to tak some lessons, I think I could make some hand of his feet, for he is a souple chield, and has a gallant instep of his ain; and sic a laced hat hasna been seen on the causeway of Middlemas this mony a day.—Ye are standing laughing there, Dick Middlemas; I would have you be sure he does not cut you out with your bonny partner yonder."

"He be—!" Middlemas was beginning a sentence which he could not have concluded with strict attention to propriety, when the master of the band summoned McFittoch to his post, by the following ireful expostulation:— "What are ye about, sir? Mind your bow-hand. How the deil d'ye think three fiddles is to keep down a bass, if yin o' them stands girning and gabbling as ye're doing? Play up, sir!"

Dick Middlemas, thus reduced to silence, continued, from his lofty station, like one of the gods of the Epicureans, to survey what passed below, without the gaieties which he witnessed being able to excite more than a smile, which seemed, however, rather to indicate a good-humoured contempt for what was passing, than a benevolent sympathy with the pleasures of others.

CHAPTER 4

Now hold thy tongue, Billy Bewick, he said,
Of peaceful talking: let me be;
But if thou art a man, as I think thou art,
Come ower the dyke and fight with me.

BORDER MINSTRELSY.

On the morning after this gay evening, the two young men were labouring together in a plot of ground behind Stevenlaw's Land, which the Doctor had converted into a garden, where he raised, with a view to pharmacy as well as botany, some rare plants, which obtained the place from the vulgar the sounding name of the Physic Garden.[9] Mr. Gray's pupils readily complied with his wishes, that they would take some care of this favourite spot, to which both contributed their labours, after which Hartley used to devote himself to the cultivation of the kitchen garden, which he had raised into this respectability from a spot not excelling a common kail-yard, while Richard Middleman did his utmost to decorate with flowers and shrubs a sort of arbour, usually called Miss Menie's bower.

At present they were both in the botanic patch of the garden, when Dick Middlemas asked Hartley why he had left the ball so soon the evening before?

"I should rather ask you," said Hartley, "what pleasure you felt in staying there?—I tell you, Dick, it is a shabby low place this Middlemas of ours. In the smallest burgh in England, every decent freeholder would have been asked if the Member gave a ball."

"What, Hartley!" said his companion, "are you, of all men, a candidate for the honour of mixing with the first-born of the earth? Mercy on us! How will canny Northumberland [throwing a true northern accent on the letter R] acquit himself? Methinks I see thee in thy pea-green suit, dancing a jig with the honourable Miss Maddie MacFudgeon, while chiefs and thanes around laugh as they would do at a hog in armour!"

---

9 The Botanic Garden is so termed by the vulgar of Edinburgh.

"You don't, or perhaps you won't, understand me." said Hartley. "I am not such a fool as to desire to be hail-fellow-well-met with these fine folks—I care as little for them as they do for me. But as they do not choose to ask us to dance, I don't see what business they have with our partners."

"Partners, said you!" answered Middlemas; "I don't think Menie is very often yours."

"As often as I ask her," answered Hartley, rather haughtily.

"Ay? Indeed?—I did not think that.—And hang me, if I think so yet." said Middlemas, with the same sarcastic tone. "I tell thee, Adam, I will bet you a bowl of punch, that Miss Gray will not dance with you the next time you ask her. All I stipulate, is to know the day."

"I will lay no bets about Miss Gray," said Hartley; "her father is my master, and I am obliged to him—I think I should act very scurvily, if I were to make her the subject of any idle debate betwixt you and me."

"Very right," replied Middlemas; "you should finish one quarrel before you begin another. Pray, saddle your pony, ride up to the gate of Loupon-height Castle, and defy the Baron to mortal combat, for having presumed to touch the fair hand of Menie Gray."

"I wish you would leave Miss Gray's name out of the question, and take your defiances to your fine folks in your own name, and see what they will say to the surgeon's apprentice."

"Speak for yourself, if you please, Mr. Adam Hartley. I was not born a clown like some folks, and should care little, if I saw it fit, to talk to the best of them at the ordinary, and make myself understood too."

"Very likely," answered Hartley, losing patience: "you are one of themselves, you know—Middlemas of that Ilk."

"You scoundrel!" said Richard, advancing on him in fury, his taunting humour entirely changed into rage.

"Stand back," said Hartley, "or you will come by the worst; if you will break rude jests, you must put up with rough answers."

"I will have satisfaction for this insult, by Heaven!"

"Why so you shall, if you insist on it," said Hartley; "but better, I think, to say no more about the matter. We have both spoken what would have been better left unsaid. I was in the wrong to say what I said to you, although you did provoke me. And now I have given you as much satisfaction as a reasonable man can ask."

"Sir," repeated Middlemas, "the satisfaction which I demand, is that of a gentleman—the Doctor has a pair of pistols.".

"And a pair of mortars also, which are heartily at your service, gentlemen," said Mr. Gray, coming forward from behind a yew hedge, where he had listened to the whole or greater part of this dispute. "A fine story it would be of my apprentices shooting each other with my own pistols! Let me see either of you fit to treat a gunshot wound, before you think of inflicting one. Go, you are both very foolish boys, and I cannot take it kind of either of you to bring the name of my daughter into such disputes as these. Hark ye, lads, ye both owe me, I think, some portion of respect, and even of gratitude—it will be a poor return, if instead of living quietly with this poor motherless girl, like brothers with a sister, you should oblige me to increase my expense, and abridge my comfort, by sending my child from me, for the few months that you are to remain here. Let me see you shake hands, and let us have no more of this nonsense."

While their master spoke in this manner, both the young men stood before him in the attitude of self-convicted criminals. At the conclusion of his rebuke, Hartley turned frankly round, and, offered his hand to his companion, who accepted it, but after a moment's hesitation. There was nothing farther passed on the subject, but the lads never resumed the same sort of intimacy which had existed betwixt them in their earlier acquaintance. On the contrary, avoiding every connexion not absolutely required by their situation, and abridging as much as possible even their indispensable intercourse in professional matters, they seemed as much estranged from each other as two persons residing in the same small house had the means of being.

As for Menie Gray, her father did not appear to entertain the least anxiety upon her account, although from his frequent and almost daily absence from home, she was exposed to constant intercourse with two handsome young men, both, it might be supposed, ambitious of pleasing her more than most parents would have deemed entirely prudent. Nor was Nurse Jamieson,—her menial situation, and her excessive partiality for her foster-son, considered,—altogether such a matron as could afford her protection. Gideon, however, knew that his daughter possessed, in its fullest extent, the upright and pure integrity of his own character, and that never father had less reason to apprehend that a daughter should deceive his confidence; and justly secure of her principles, he overlooked the danger to which he exposed her feelings and affections.

The intercourse betwixt Menie and the young men seemed now of a guarded kind on all sides. Their meeting was only at meals, and Miss Gray was at pains, perhaps by her father's recommendation, to treat them with. the same degree of attention. This, however, was no easy matter; for Hartley became so retiring, cold, and formal, that it was impossible for her to sustain any prolonged intercourse with him; whereas Middlemas, perfectly at his ease, sustained his part as formerly upon all occasions that occurred, and without appearing to press his intimacy assiduously, seemed nevertheless to retain the complete possession of it.

The time drew nigh at length when the young men, freed from the engagements of their indentures, must look to play their own independent part in the world. Mr. Gray informed Richard Middlemas that he had written pressingly upon the subject to Moncada, and that more than once, but had not yet received an answer; nor did he presume to offer his own advice, until the pleasure of his grandfather should be known. Richard seemed to endure this suspense with more patience than the Doctor thought belonged naturally to his character. He asked no questions—stated no conjectures—showed no anxiety, but seemed to await with patience the turn which events should take. "My young gentleman," thought Mr. Gray, "has either fixed on some course in his own mind, or he is about to be more tractable than some points of his character have led me to expect."

In fact, Richard had made an experiment on this inflexible relative, by sending Mr. Moncada a letter full of duty, and affection, and gratitude, desiring to be permitted to correspond with him in person, and promising to be guided in every particular by his will. The answer to this appeal was his own letter returned, with a note from the bankers whose cover had been used, saying, that any future attempt to intrude on Mr. Moncada, would put a final period to their remittances.

While things were in this situation in Stevenlaw's Land, Adam Hartley one evening, contrary to his custom for several months, sought a private interview with his fellow-apprentice. He found him in the little arbour, and could not omit observing, that Dick Middlemas, on his appearance, shoved into his bosom a small packet, as if afraid of its being seen, and snatching up a hoe, began to work with great devotion, like one who wished to have it thought that his whole soul was in his occupation.

"I wished to speak with you, Mr. Middlemas," said Hartley; "but I fear I interrupt you."

"Not in the least,'" said the other, laying down his hoe; "I was only scratching up the weeds which the late showers have made rush up so numerously. I am at your service."

Hartley proceeded to the arbour, and seated himself. Richard imitated his example, and seemed to wait for the proposed communication.

"I have had an interesting communication with Mr. Gray"—said Hartley, and there stopped, like one who finds himself entering upon a difficult task.

"I hope the explanation has been satisfactory?" said Middlemas.

"You shall judge.—Doctor Gray was pleased to say something to me very civil about my proficiency in the duties of our profession; and, to my great astonishment, asked me, whether, as he was now becoming old, I had any particular objection to continue in my present situation, but with some pecuniary advantages, for two years longer; at the end of which he promised to me that I should enter into partnership with him."

"Mr. Gray is an undoubted judge," said Middlemas, "what person will best suit him as a professional assistant. The business may be worth £200 a-year, and an active assistant might go nigh to double it, by riding Strath-Devan and the Carse. No great subject for division after all, Mr. Hartley."

"But," continued Hartley, "that is not all. The Doctor says—he proposes—in short, if I can render myself agreeable, in the course of these two years, to Miss Menie Gray, he proposes, that when they terminate, I should become his son as well as his partner."

As he spoke, he kept his eye fixed on Richard's face, which was for a moment, strongly agitated; but instantly recovering, he answered, in a tone where pique and offended pride vainly endeavoured to disguise themselves under an affectation of indifference. "Well, Master Adam, I cannot but wish you joy of the patriarchal arrangement. You have served five years for a professional diploma—a sort of Leah, that privilege of killing and curing. Now you begin a new course of servitude for a lovely Rachel. Undoubtedly—perhaps it is rude in me to ask—but undoubtedly you have accepted so flattering an arrangement?"

"You cannot but recollect there was a condition annexed," said Hartley, gravely.

"That of rendering yourself acceptable to a girl you have known for so many years?" said Middlemas with a half-suppressed sneer. "No great difficulty in that, I should think, for such a person as Mr. Hartley, with Doctor Gray's favour to back him. No, no-there could be no great obstacle there."

"Both you and I know the contrary, Mr. Middlemas," said Hartley, very seriously.

"I know?—How should I know any thing more than yourself about the state of Miss Gray's inclinations?" said Middlemas. "I am sure we have had equal access to know them."

"Perhaps so; but some know better how to avail themselves of opportunities. Mr. Middlemas, I have long suspected that you have had the inestimable advantages of possessing Miss Gray's affections, and"—

"I?" interrupted Middlemas; "you are jesting, or you are jealous. You do yourself less, and me more, than justice; but the compliment is so great, that I am obliged to you for the mistake."

"That you may know," answered Hartley, "I do not speak either by guess, or from what you call jealousy, I tell you frankly, that Menie Gray herself told me the state of her affections. I naturally communicated to her the discourse I had with her father. I told her I was but too well convinced that at the present moment I did not possess that interest in her heart, which alone might entitle me to request her acquiescence in the views which her father's goodness held out to me; but I entreated her not at once to decide against me, but give me an opportunity to make way in her affections, if possible, trusting that time, and the services which I should render to her father, might have an ultimate effect in my favour."

"A most natural and modest request. But what did the young lady say in reply?"

"She is a noble-hearted girl, Richard Middlemas; and for her frankness alone, even without her beauty and her good sense, deserves an emperor. I cannot express the graceful modesty with which she told me, that she knew too well the kindliness, as she was pleased to call it, of my heart, to expose me to the protracted pain of an unrequited passion. She candidly informed me that she had been long engaged to you in secret—that you had exchanged portraits;—and though without her father's consent she would never become yours, yet she felt it impossible that she should ever so far change her sentiments as to afford the most distant prospect of success to another."

"Upon my word," said Middlemas, "she has been extremely candid indeed, and I am very much obliged to her!"

"And upon *my* honest word, Mr. Middlemas," returned Hartley, "you do Miss Gray the greatest injustice—nay, you are ungrateful to her, if you are displeased at her making this declaration. She loves you as a woman loves the first object of her affection—she loves you better"—He stopped, and Middlemas completed the sentence.

"Better than I deserve, perhaps?—Faith, it may well be so, and I love her dearly in return. But after all, you know, the secret was mine as well as hers, and it would have been better that she had consulted me before making it public."

"Mr. Middlemas," said Hartley, earnestly, "if the least of this feeling, on your part, arises from the apprehension that your secret is less safe because it is in my keeping, I can assure you that such is my grateful sense of Miss Gray's goodness, in communicating, to save me pain, an affair of such delicacy to herself and you, that wild horses should tear me limb from limb before they forced a word of it from my lips."

"Nay, nay, my dear friend," said Middlemas, with a frankness of manner indicating a cordiality that had not existed between them for some time, "you must allow me to be a little jealous in my turn. Your true lover cannot have a title to the name, unless he be sometimes unreasonable; and somehow, it seems odd she should have chosen for a confidant one whom I have often thought a formidable rival; and yet I am so far from being displeased, that I do not know that the dear sensible girl could after all have made a better choice. It is time that the foolish coldness between us should be ended, as you must be sensible that its real cause lay in our rivalry. I have much need of good advice, and who can give it to me better than the old companion, whose soundness of judgment I have always envied, even when some injudicious friends have given me credit for quicker parts?"

Hartley accepted Richard's proffered hand, but without any of the buoyancy of spirit with which it was offered.

"I do not intend," he said, "to remain many days in this place, perhaps not very many hours. But if, in the meanwhile, I can benefit you, by advice or otherwise, you may fully command me. It is the only mode in which I can be of service to Menie Gray."

"Love my mistress, love me; a happy *pendant* to the old proverb, Love me, love my dog. Well, then, for Menie Gray's sake, if not for Dick Middlemas's, (plague on that vulgar tell-tale name,) will you, that are a stander-by, tell us, who are the unlucky players, what you think of this game of ours?"

"How can you ask such a question, when the field lies so fair before you? I am sure that Dr. Gray would retain you as his assistant upon the same terms which he proposed to me. You are the better match, in all worldly respects, for his daughter, having some capital to begin the world with."

"All true—but methinks Mr. Gray has showed no great predilection for me in this matter."

"If he has done injustice to your indisputable merit," said Hartley, dryly, "the preference of his daughter has more than atoned for it."

"Unquestionably; and dearly, therefore, do I love her; otherwise, Adam, I am not a person to grasp at the leavings of other people."

"Richard," replied Hartley, "that pride of yours, if you do not check it, will render you both ungrateful and miserable. Mr. Gray's ideas are most friendly. He told me plainly that his choice of me as an assistant, and as a member of his family, had been a long time balanced by his early affection for you, until he thought he had remarked in you a decisive discontent with such limited prospects as his offer contained, and a desire to go abroad into the world, and push, as it is called, your fortune. He said, that although it was very probable that you might love his daughter well enough to relinquish these ambitious ideas for her sake, yet the demons of Ambition and Avarice would return after the exorciser Love had exhausted the force of his spells, and then he thought he would have just reason to be anxious for his daughter's happiness."

"By my faith, the worthy senior speaks scholarly and wisely," answered Richard—"I did not think he had been so clear-sighted. To say the truth, but for the beautiful Menie Gray, I should feel like a mill-horse, walking my daily round in this dull country, while other gay rovers are trying how the world will receive them. For instance, where do you yourself go?"

"A cousin of my mother's commands a ship in the Company's service. I intend to go with him as surgeon's mate. If I like the sea service, I will continue in it; if not, I will enter some other line." This Hartley said with a sigh.

"To India!" answered Richard; "Happy dog—to India! You may well bear with equanimity all disappointments sustained on this side of the globe. Oh, Delhi! oh, Golconda! have your names no power to conjure down idle recollections?—India, where gold is won by steel; where a brave man cannot pitch his desire for fame and wealth so high, but that he may realize it, if he have fortune to his friend? Is it possible that the bold adventurer can fix his thoughts on you, and still be dejected at the thoughts that a bonny blue-eyed lass looked favourably on a less lucky fellow than himself? Can this be?"

"Less lucky?" said Hartley. "Can you, the accepted lover of Menie Gray, speak in that tone, even though it be in jest!"

"Nay, Adam," said Richard, "don't be angry with me, because, being thus far successful, I rate my good fortune not quite so rapturously as perhaps you do, who have missed the luck of it. Your philosophy should tell you, that the object which we attain, or are sure of attaining, loses, perhaps, even by that very certainty, a little of the extravagant and ideal value, which attached to it while the object of feverish hopes and aguish fears. But for all that, I cannot live without my sweet Menie. I would wed her to-morrow, with all my soul, without thinking a minute on the clog which so early a marriage would fasten on our heels. But to spend two additional years in this infernal wilderness, cruising after crowns and half-crowns, when worse men are making lacs and crores of rupees—It is a sad falling off, Adam. Counsel me, my friend,—can you not suggest some mode of getting off from these two years of destined dulness?"

"Not I," replied Hartley, scarce repressing his displeasure; "and if I could induce Dr. Gray to dispense with so reasonable a condition, I should be very sorry to do so. You are but twenty-one, and if such a period of probation was, in the Doctor's prudence, judged necessary for me, who am full two years older, I have no idea that he will dispense with it in yours."

"Perhaps not," replied Middlemas; "but do you not think that these two, or call them three, years of probation, had better be spent in India, where much may be done in a little while, than here, where nothing can be done save just enough to get salt to our broth, or broth to our salt? Methinks I have a natural turn for India, and so I ought. My father was a soldier, by the conjecture of all who saw him, and gave me a love of the sword, and an arm to use one. My mother's father was a rich trafficker, who loved wealth, I warrant me, and knew how to get it. This petty two hundred a-year, with its miserable and precarious possibilities, to be shared with the old gentleman, sounds in the ears of one like me, who have the world for the winning, and a sword to cut my way through it, like something little better than a decent kind of beggary. Menie is in herself a gem—a diamond—I admit it. But then, one would not set such a precious jewel in lead or popper, but in pure gold; ay, and add a circlet of brilliants to set it off with. Be a good fellow, Adam, and undertake the setting my project in proper colours before the Doctor. I am sure, the wisest thing for him and Menie both, is to permit me to spend this short time of probation in the land of cowries. I am sure my heart will be there at any rate, and while I am bleeding some bumpkin for an inflammation, I shall be in fancy relieving some nabob, or rajahpoot, of his plethora of wealth.

Come—will you assist, will you be auxiliary? Ten chances but you plead your own cause, man, for I may be brought up by a sabre, or a bow-string, before I make my pack up; then your road to Menie will be free and open, and, as you will be possessed of the situation of comforter *ex officio*, you may take her 'with the tear in her ee,' as old saws advise."

"Mr. Richard Middlemas," said Hartley, "I wish it were possible for me to tell you, in the few words which I intend to bestow on you, whether I pity you or despise you, the most. Heaven has placed happiness, competence, and content within your power, and you are willing to cast them away, to gratify ambition and avarice. Were I to give any advice on this subject either to Dr. Gray or his daughter, it would be to break of all connexion with a man, who, however clever by nature, may soon show himself a fool, and however honestly brought up, may also, upon temptation, prove himself a villain.—You may lay aside the sneer, which is designed to be a sarcastic smile. I will not attempt to do this, because I am convinced that my advice would be of no use, unless it could come unattended with suspicion of my motives. I will hasten my departure from this house, that we may not meet again; and I will leave it to God Almighty to protect honesty and innocence against the dangers which must attend vanity and folly." So saying, he turned contemptuously from the youthful votary of ambition, and left the garden.

"Stop," said Middlemas, struck with the picture which had been held up to his conscience—"Stop, Adam Hartley, and I will confess to you"—But his words were uttered in a faint and hesitating manner, and either never reached Hartley's ear, or failed in changing his purpose of departure.

When he was out of the garden, Middlemas began to recall his usual boldness of disposition—"Had he staid a moment longer," he said, "I would have turned Papist, and made him my ghostly confessor. The yeomanly churl!—I would give something to know how he has got such a hank over me. What are Menie Gray's engagements to him? She has given him his answer, and what right has he to come betwixt her and me? If old Moncada had done a grandfather's duty, and made suitable settlements on me, this plan of marrying the sweet girl, and settling here in her native place, might have done well enough. But to live the life of the poor drudge her father—to be at the command and call of every boor for twenty miles round!—why, the labours of a higgler, who travels scores of miles to barter pins, ribbons, snuff and tobacco, against the housewife's private stock of eggs, mort-skins, and tallow, is more profitable, less laborious, and faith I think, equally respectable. No, no,—unless I can find wealth nearer home, I will seek it where every one can have it for the gathering; and so I will down to the Swan Inn, and hold a final consultation with my friend."

CHAPTER 5

The friend whom Middlemas expected to meet at the Swan, was a person already mentioned in this history by the name of Tom Hillary, bred an attorney's clerk in the ancient town of Novum Castrum—*doctus utriusque juris*, as far as a few months in the service of Mr. Lawford, Town-clerk of Middlemas, could render him so. The last mention that we made of this gentleman, was when his gold-laced hat veiled its splendour before the fresher mounted beavers of the 'prentices of Dr. Gray. That was now about five years since, and it was within six months that he had made his appearance in Middlemas, a very different sort of personage from that which he seemed at his departure.

He was now called Captain; his dress was regimental, and his language martial. He appeared to have plenty of cash, for he not only, to the great surprise of the parties, paid certain old debts, which he had left unsettled behind him, and that notwithstanding his having, as his old practice told. him, a good defence of prescription, but even sent the minister a guinea, to the assistance of the parish poor. These acts of justice and benevolence were bruited abroad greatly to the honour of one, who, so long absent, had neither forgotten his just debts, nor hardened his heart against the cries of the needy. His merits were thought the higher, when it was understood he had served the Honourable East India Company—that wonderful company of merchants, who may indeed, with the strictest propriety, be termed princes. It was about the middle of the eighteenth century, and the directors in Leadenhall Street were silently laying the foundation of that immense empire, which afterwards rose like an exhalation, and now astonishes Europe, as well as Asia, with its formidable extent, and stupendous strength. Britain had now begun to lend a wondering ear to the account of battles fought, and cities won, in the East; and was surprised by the return of individuals who had left their native country as adventurers, but now reappeared there surrounded by Oriental wealth and Oriental luxury, which dimmed even the splendour of the most wealthy of the British nobility. In this new-found El Dorada, Hillary had, it seems, been a labourer, and, if he told truth, to some purpose, though he was far from having completed the harvest which he meditated. He spoke, indeed, of making investments, and, as a mere matter of fancy, he consulted his old master, Clerk Lawford, concerning the purchase of a moorland farm of three thousand acres, for which he would be content to give three or four thousand guineas, providing the game was plenty, and the trouting in the brook such as had been represented by advertisement. But he did not wish to make any extensive landed purchase at present. It was necessary to keep up his interest in Leadenhall Street; and in that view, it would be impolitic to part with his India stock and India bonds. In short, it was folly to think of settling on a poor thousand or twelve hundred a year, when one was in the prime of life, and had no liver complaint; and so he was determined to double the Cape once again, ere he retired to the chimney corner for life. All he wished was, to pick up a few clever fellows for his regiment, or rather for his own company; and as in all his travels he had never seen finer fellows than about Middlemas, he was willing to give them the preference in completing his levy. In fact, it was making men of them at once, for a few white faces never failed to strike terror into these black rascals; and then, not to mention the good things that were going at the storming of a Pettah, or the plundering of a Pagoda, most of these tawny dogs carried so much treasure about their persons, that a won battle was equal to a min e of gold to the victors.

The natives of Middlemas listened to the noble Captain's marvels with different feelings, as their temperaments were saturnine or sanguine. But none could deny that such things had been; and, as the narrator was known to be a bold dashing fellow, possessed of some abilities, and according to the general opinion, not likely to be withheld by any peculiar scruples of conscience, there was no giving any good reason why Hillary should not have been as successful as others in the field, which India, agitated as it was by war and intestine disorders, seemed to offer to every enterprising adventurer. He was accordingly received by his old acquaintances at Middlemas rather with the respect due to his supposed wealth, than in a manner corresponding with his former humble pretensions.

Some of the notables of the village did indeed keep aloof. Among these, the chief was Dr. Gray, who was an enemy to every thing that approached to fanfaronade, and knew enough of the world to lay it down as a sort of general rule, that he who talks a great deal of fighting is seldom a brave soldier, and he who always speaks about wealth is seldom a rich man at bottom. Clerk Lawford was also shy, notwithstanding his *communings* with Hillary upon the subject of his intended purchase. The coolness of the Captain's old employer towards him was by some supposed to arise out of certain circumstances attending their former connexion; but as the Clerk himself never explained what these were, it is unnecessary to make any conjectures upon the subject.

Richard Middlemas very naturally renewed his intimacy with his former comrade, and it was from Hillary's conversation, that he had adopted the enthusiasm respecting India, which we have heard him express. It was indeed impossible for a youth, at once inexperienced in the world, and possessed of a most sanguine disposition, to listen without sympathy to the glowing descriptions of Hillary, who, though only a recruiting captain, had all the eloquence of a recruiting sergeant. Palaces rose like mushrooms in his descriptions; groves of lofty trees, and aromatic shrubs unknown to the chilly soils of Europe, were tenanted by every object of the chase, from the royal tiger down to the jackal. The luxuries of a natch, and the peculiar Oriental beauty of the enchantresses who perfumed their voluptuous Eastern domes, for the pleasure of the haughty English conquerors, were no less attractive than the battles and sieges on which the Captain at other times expatiated. Not a stream did he mention but flowed over sands of gold, and not a palace that was inferior to those of the celebrated Fata Morgana. His descriptions seemed steeped in odours, and his every phrase perfumed in ottar of roses. The interviews at which these descriptions took place, often ended in a bottle of choicer wine than the Swan Inn afforded, with some other appendages of the table, which the Captain, who was a *bon-vivant*, had procured from Edinburgh. From this good cheer Middlemas was doomed to retire to the homely evening meal of his master, where not all the simple beauties of Menie were able to overcome his disgust at the coarseness of the provisions, or his unwillingness to answer questions concerning the diseases of the wretched peasants who were subjected to his inspection.

Richard's hopes of being acknowledged by his father had long since vanished, and the rough repulse and subsequent neglect on the part of Moncada, had satisfied him that his grandfather was inexorable, and that neither then, nor at any future time, did he mean to realize the visions which Nurse Jamieson's splendid figments had encouraged him to entertain. Ambition, however, was not lulled to sleep, though it was no longer nourished by the same hopes which had at first awakened it. The Indian Captain's lavish oratory supplied the themes which had been at first derived from the legends of the nursery; the exploits of a Lawrence and a Clive, as well as the magnificent opportunities of acquiring wealth to which these exploits opened the road, disturbed the slumbers of the young adventurer. There was nothing to counteract these except his love for Menie Gray, and the engagements into which it had led him. But his addresses had been paid to Menie as much for the gratification of his vanity, as from any decided passion for that innocent and guileless being. He was desirous of carrying off the prize, for which Hartley, whom he never loved, had the courage to contend with him. Then Menie Gray had been beheld with admiration by men his superiors in rank and fortune, but with whom his ambition incited him to dispute the prize. No doubt, though urged to play the gallant at first rather from vanity than any other cause, the frankness and modesty with which his suit was admitted, made their natural impression on his heart. He was grateful to the beautiful creature, who acknowledged the superiority of his person and accomplishments, and fancied himself as devotedly attached to her, as her personal charms and mental merits would have rendered any one who was less vain or selfish than her lover. Still his passion for the surgeon's daughter ought not, he prudentially determined, to bear more than its due weight in a case so very important as the determining his line of life; and this he smoothed over to his conscience, by repeating to himself, that Menie's interest was as essentially concerned as his own, in postponing their marriage to the establishment of his fortune. How many young couples had been ruined by a premature union!

The contemptuous conduct of Hartley in their last interview, had done something to shake his comrade's confidence in the truth of this reasoning, and to lead him to suspect that he was playing a very sordid and unmanly part, in trifling with the happiness of this amiable and unfortunate young woman. It was in this doubtful humour that he repaired to the Swan Inn, where he was anxiously expected by his friend the Captain.

When they were comfortably seated over a bottle of Paxarete, Middlemas began, with characteristical caution, to sound his friend about the ease or difficulty with which an individual, desirous of entering the Company's service, might have an opportunity of getting a commission. If Hillary had answered truly, he would have replied, that it was extremely easy; for, at that time, the East India service presented no charms to that superior class of people who have since struggled for admittance under its banners. But the worthy Captain replied, that though, in the general case, it might be difficult for a young man to obtain a commission, without serving for some years as a cadet, yet, under his own protection, a young man entering his regiment, and fitted for such a situation, might be sure of an ensigncy, if not a lieutenancy, as soon as ever they set foot in India. "If you, my dear fellow," continued he, extending his hand to Middlemas, "would think of changing sheep-head broth and haggis for mulagatawny and curry, I can only say, that though it is indispensable that you should enter the service at first simply as a cadet, yet, by—; you should live like a brother on the passage with me; and no sooner were we through the surf at Madras, than I would put you in the way of acquiring both wealth and glory. You have, I think, some trifle of money—a couple of thousands or so?"

"About a thousand or twelve hundred," said Richard, affecting the indifference of his companion, but feeling privately humbled by the scantiness of his resources.

"It is quite as much as you will find necessary for the outfit and passage," said his adviser; "and, indeed, if you had not a farthing, it would be the same thing; for if I once say to a friend, I'll help you, Tom Hillary is not the man to start for fear of the cowries. However, it is as well you have something of a capital of your own to begin upon."

"Yes," replied the proselyte. "I should not like to be a burden on any one. I have some thoughts, to tell you the truth, to marry before I leave Britain; and in that case, you know, cash will be necessary, whether my wife goes out with us, or remains behind, till she hear how luck goes with me. So, after all, I may have to borrow a few hundreds of you."

"What the devil is that you say, Dick, about marrying and giving in marriage?" replied his friend. "What can put it into the head of a gallant young fellow like you, just rising twenty-one, and six feet high on your stocking-soles, to make a slave of yourself for life? No, no, Dick, that will never do. Remember the old song,

'Bachelor Bluff, bachelor Bluff,
    Hey for a heart that is rugged and tough!'"

"Ay, ay, that sounds very well," replied Middlemas; "but then one must shake off a number of old recollections."

"The sooner the better, Dick; old recollections are like old clothes, and should be sent off by wholesale; they only take up room in one's wardrobe, and it would be old-fashioned to wear them. But you look grave upon it. Who the devil is it that has made such a hole in your heart?"

"Pshaw!" answered Middlemas, "I'm sure you must remember—Menie—my master's daughter."

"What, Miss Green, the old pottercarrier's daughter?—a likely girl enough, I think."

"My master is a surgeon," said Richard, "not an apothecary, and his name is Gray."

"Ay, ay, Green or Gray—what does it signify? He sells his own drugs, I think, which we in the south call being a pottercarrier. The girl is a likely girl enough for a Scottish ball-room. But is she up to any thing? Has she any *nouz*?"

"Why, she is a sensible girl, save in loving me," answered Richard; "and that, as Benedict says, is no proof of her wisdom, and no great argument of her folly."

"But has she spirit—spunk—dash—a spice of the devil about her?"

"Not a penny-weight—the kindest, simplest, and most manageable of human beings," answered the lover.

"She won't do then," said the monitor, in a decisive tone. "I am sorry for it, Dick: but she will never do. There are some women in the world that can bear their share in the bustling life we live in India—ay, and I have known some of

70

them drag forward husbands that would otherwise have stuck fast in the mud till the day of judgment. Heaven knows how they paid the turnpikes they pushed them through! But these were none of your simple Susans, that think their eyes are good for nothing but to look at their husbands, or their fingers but to sew baby-clothes. Depend on it, you must give up your matrimony, or your views of preferment. If you wilfully tie a clog round your throat, never think of running a race; but do not suppose that your breaking off with the lass will make any very terrible catastrophe. A scene there may be at parting; but you will soon forget her among the native girls, and she will fall in love with Mr. Tapeitout, the minister's assistant and successor. She is not goods for the Indian market, I assure you."

Among the capricious weaknesses of humanity, that one is particularly remarkable which inclines us to esteem persons and things not by their real value, or even by our own judgment, so much as by the opinion of others, who are often very incompetent judges. Dick Middlemas had been urged forward, in his suit to Menie Gray, by his observing how much her partner, a booby laird, had been captivated by her; and she was now lowered in his esteem, because an impudent low-lived coxcomb had presumed to talk of her with disparagement. Either of these worthy gentlemen would have been as capable of enjoying the beauties of Homer, as judging of the merits of Menie Gray.

Indeed the ascendency which this bold-talking, promise-making soldier had acquired over Dick Middlemas, wilful as he was in general, was of a despotic nature; because the Captain, though greatly inferior in information and talent to the youth whose opinions he swayed, had skill in suggesting those tempting views of rank and wealth, to which Richard's imagination had been from childhood most accessible. One promise he exacted from Middlemas, as a condition of the services which he was to render him—It was absolute silence on the subject of his destination for India, and the views upon which it took place. "My recruits," said the Captain, "have been all marched off for the depot at the Isle of Wight; and I want to leave Scotland, and particularly this little burgh, without being worried to death, of which I must despair, should it come to be known that I can provide young griffins, as we call them, with commissions. Gad, I should carry off all the first-born of Middlemas as cadets, and none are so scrupulous as I am about making promises. I am as trusty as a Trojan for that; and you know I cannot do that for every one which I would for an old friend like Dick Middlemas."

Dick promised secrecy, and it was agreed that the two friends should not even leave the burgh in company, but that the Captain should set off first, and his recruit should join him at Edinburgh, where his enlistment might be attested; and then they were to travel together to town, and arrange matters for their Indian voyage.

Notwithstanding the definitive arrangement which was thus made for his departure, Middlemas thought from time to time with anxiety and regret about quitting Menie Gray, after the engagement which had passed between them. The resolution was taken, however; the blow was necessarily to be struck; and her ungrateful lover, long since determined against the life of domestic happiness, which he might have enjoyed had his views been better regulated, was now occupied with the means, not indeed of breaking off with her entirely, but of postponing all thoughts of their union until the success of his expedition to India.

He might have spared himself all anxiety on this last subject. The wealth of that India to which he was bound would not have bribed Menie Gray to have left her father's roof against her father's commands; still less when, deprived of his two assistants, he must be reduced to the necessity of continued exertion in his declining life, and therefore might have accounted himself altogether deserted, had his daughter departed from him at the same time. But though it would have been her unalterable determination not to accept any proposal of an immediate union of their fortunes, Menie could not, with all a lover's power of self-deception, succeed in persuading herself to be satisfied with Richard's conduct towards her. Modesty, and a becoming pride, prevented her from seeming to notice, but could not prevent her from bitterly feeling, that her lover was preferring the pursuits of ambition to the humble lot which he might have shared with her, and which promised content at least, if not wealth.

"If he had loved me as he pretended," such was the unwilling conviction that rose on her mind, "my father would surely not have ultimately refused him the same terms which he held out to Hartley. His objections would have given way to my happiness, nay, to Richard's importunities, which would have removed his suspicions of the unsettled cast of his disposition. But I fear—I fear Richard hardly thought the terms proposed were worthy of his acceptance. Would it not have been natural too, that he should have asked me, engaged as we stand to each other, to have united our faith before his quitting Europe, when I might either have remained here with my father, or accompanied him to India, in quest of that fortune which he is so eagerly pushing for? It would have been wrong—very wrong—in me to have consented to such a proposal, unless my father had authorised it; but surely it would have been natural that Richard should have offered it? Alas! men do not know how to love like women! Their attachment is only one of a thousand other passions and predilections,—they are daily engaged in pleasures which blunt their feelings, and in business which distracts them. We—we sit at home to weep, and to think how coldly our affections are repaid!"

The time was now arrived at which Richard Middlemas had a right to demand the property vested in the hands of the Town-clerk and Doctor Gray.

He did so, and received it accordingly. His late guardian naturally enquired what views he had formed in entering on life? The imagination, of the ambitious aspirant saw in this simple question a desire, on the part of the worthy man, to offer, and perhaps press upon him, the same proposal which he had made to Hartley. He hastened, therefore, to answer dryly, that he had some hopes held out to him which he was not at liberty to communicate; but that the instant he reached London, he would write to the guardian of his youth, and acquaint him with the nature of his prospects, which he was happy to say were rather of a pleasing character.

Gideon, who supposed that at this critical period of his life, the father, or grandfather, of the young man might perhaps have intimated a disposition to open some intercourse with him, only replied,—"You have been the child of mystery, Richard; and as you came to me, so you leave me. Then, I was ignorant from whence you came, and now, I know not whither you are, going. It is not, perhaps, a very favourable point in your horoscope, that every thing connected with you is a secret. But as I shall always think with kindness on him whom I have known so long, so when you remember the old man, you ought not to forget that he has done his duty to you, to the extent of his means and power, and taught you that noble profession, by means of which, wherever your lot casts you, you may always gain your bread, and alleviate at the same time, the distresses of your fellow creatures." Middlemas was excited by the simple kindness of his master, and poured forth his thanks with the greater profusion, that he was free from the terror of the emblematical collar and chain, which a moment before seemed to glisten in the hand of his guardian, and gape to enclose his neck.

"One word more," said Mr. Gray, producing a small ring-case. "This valuable ring was forced upon me by your unfortunate mother. I have no right to it, having been amply paid for my services; and I only accepted it with the purpose of keeping it for you till this moment should arrive. It may be useful, perhaps, should there occur any question about your identity."

"Thanks, once more, my more than father, for this precious relic, which, may indeed be useful. You shall be repaid, if India has diamonds left."

"India, and diamonds!" said Gray. "Is your head turned, child?"

"I mean," stammered Middlemas, "if London has any Indian diamonds."

"Pooh! you foolish lad," answered Gray, "how should you buy diamonds, or what should I do with them, if you gave me ever so many? Get you gone with you while I am angry."—The tears were glistening in the old man's eyes—"If I get pleased with you again, I shall not know how to part with you."

The parting of Middlemas with poor Menie was yet more affecting. Her sorrow revived in his mind all the liveliness of a first love, and he redeemed his character for sincere attachment, by not only imploring an instant union, but even going so far as to propose renouncing his more splendid prospects, and sharing Mr. Gray's humble toil, if by doing so he could secure his daughter's hand. But though there was consolation in this testimony of her lover's faith, Menie Gray was not so unwise as to accept of sacrifices which might afterwards have been repented of.

"No, Richard," she said, "it seldom ends happily when people alter, in a moment of agitated feeling, plans which might have been adopted under mature deliberation. I have long seen that your views were extended far beyond so humble a station as this place affords promise of. It is natural they should do so, considering that the circumstances of your birth seemed connected with riches and with rank. Go, then, seek that riches and rank. It is possible your mind may be changed in the pursuit, and if so, think no more about Menie Gray. But if it should be otherwise, we may meet again, and do not believe for a moment that there can be a change in Menie Gray's feelings towards you."

At this interview, much more was said than it is necessary to repeat, much more thought than was actually said. Nurse Jamieson, in whose chamber it took place, folded her *bairns*, as she called them, in her arms, and declared that Heaven had made them for each other, and that she would not ask of Heaven to live beyond the day when she should see them bridegroom and bride.

At length it became necessary that the parting scene should end; and Richard Middlemas, mounting a horse which he had hired for the journey, set off for Edinburgh, to which metropolis he had already forwarded his heavy baggage. Upon the road the idea more than once occurred to him, that even, yet he had better return to Middlemas, and secure his happiness by uniting himself at once to Menie Gray, and to humble competence. But from the moment that he rejoined his friend Hillary at their appointed place of rendezvous, he became ashamed even to hint at any change of purpose; and his late excited feelings were forgotten, unless in so far as they confirmed his resolution, that as soon as he had attained a certain portion of wealth and consequence, he would haste to share them with Menie Gray. Yet his gratitude to her father did not appear to have slumbered, if we may judge from the gift of a very handsome cornelian seal, set in gold, and bearing engraved upon it Gules, a lion rampant within a bordure Or, which was carefully despatched to Stevenlaw's Land, Middlemas, with a suitable letter. Menie knew the hand-writing and watched her father's looks as he read it, thinking, perhaps, that it had turned on a different topic. Her father pshawed and poohed a good deal when he had finished the billet, and examined the seal.

"Dick Middlemas," he said, "is but a fool after all, Menie. I am sure I am not like to forget him, that he should send me a token of remembrance; add if he would be so absurd, could he not have sent me the improved lithotomical apparatus? And what have I, Gideon Gray, to do with the arms of my Lord Gray?—No, no,—my old silver stamp, with the double G upon it, will serve my turn—But put the bonnie dye [10] away, Menie, my dear—it was kindly meant at any rate."

The reader cannot doubt that the seal was safely and carefully preserved.

---

10 "Pretty Toy"

CHAPTER 6

A lazar-house it seemed, wherein were laid
Numbers of all diseased.

MILTON.

After the Captain had finished his business, amongst which he did not forget to have his recruit regularly attested, as a candidate for glory in the service of the Honourable East India Company, the friends left Edinburgh. From thence they got a passage by sea to Newcastle, where Hillary had also some regimental affairs to transact, before he joined his regiment. At Newcastle the Captain had the good luck to find a small brig, commanded by an old acquaintance and school-fellow, which was just about to sail for the Isle of Wight. "I have arranged for our passage with him," he said to Middlemas— "for when you are at the depot, you can learn a little of your duty, which cannot be so well taught on board of ship, and then I will find it easier to have you promoted."

"Do you mean," said Richard, "that I am to stay at the Isle of Wight all the time that you are jigging it away in London?"

"Ay, indeed do I," said his comrade, "and it's best for you too; whatever business you have in London, I can do it for you as well, or something better than yourself."

"But I choose to transact my own business myself, Captain Hillary,' said Richard.

"Then you ought to have remained your own master, Mr. Cadet Middlemas. At present you are an enlisted recruit of the Honourable East India Company; I am your officer, and should you hesitate to follow me aboard, why, you foolish fellow, I could have you sent on board in hand-cuffs."

This was jestingly spoken; but yet there was something in the tone which hurt Middlemas's pride and alarmed his fears. He had observed of late, that his friend, especially when in company of others, talked to him with an air of command or superiority, difficult to be endured, and yet so closely allied to the freedom often exercised betwixt two intimates, that he could not find any proper mode of rebuffing, or resenting it. Such manifestations of authority were usually followed by an instant renewal of their intimacy; but in the present case that did not so speedily ensue.

Middlemas, indeed, consented to go with his companion to the Isle of Wight, perhaps because if he should quarrel with him, the whole plan of his Indian voyage, and all the hopes built upon it, must fall to the ground. But he altered his purpose of intrusting his comrade with his little fortune, to lay out as his occasions might require, and resolved himself to overlook the expenditure of his money, which, in the form of Bank of England notes, was safely deposited in his travelling trunk. Captain Hillary, finding that some hint he had thrown out on this subject was disregarded, appeared to think no more about it.

The voyage was performed with safety and celerity; and having coasted the shores of that beautiful island, which he who once sees never forgets, through whatever part of the world his future path may lead him, the vessel was soon anchored off the little town of Ryde; and, as the waves were uncommonly still, Richard felt the sickness diminish, which, for a considerable part of the passage, had occupied his attention more than any thing else.

The master of the brig, in honour to his passengers, and affection to his old school-fellow, had formed an awning upon deck, and proposed to have the pleasure of giving them a little treat before they left his vessel. Lobscous, sea-pie, and other delicacies of a naval description, had been provided in a quantity far disproportionate to the number of the guests. But the punch which succeeded was of excellent quality, and portentously strong. Captain Hillary pushed it round, and insisted upon his companion taking his full share in the merry bout, the rather that, as he facetiously said, there had been some dryness between them, which good liquor would be sovereign in removing. He renewed, with additional splendours, the various panoramic scenes of India and Indian adventures, which had first excited the ambition of Middlemas, and assured him, that even if he should not be able to get him a commission instantly, yet a short delay would only give him time to become better acquainted with his military duties; and Middlemas was too much elevated by the liquor he had drank to see any difficulty which could oppose itself to his fortunes. Whether those who shared in the compotation were more seasoned topers—whether Middlemas drank more than they—or whether, as he himself afterwards suspected, his cup had been drugged, like those of King Duncan's body-guard, it is certain that, on this occasion, he passed with unusual rapidity, through all the different phases of the respectable state of drunkenness—laughed, sung, whooped, and hallooed, was maudlin in his fondness, and frantic in his wrath, and at length fell into a fast and imperturbable sleep.

The effect of the liquor displayed itself, as usual, in a hundred wild dreams of parched deserts, and of serpents whose bite inflicted the most intolerable thirst—of the suffering of the Indian on the death-stake—and the torments of the infernal regions themselves; when at length he awakened, and it appeared that the latter vision was in fact realized. The sounds which had at first influenced his dreams, and at length broken his slumbers, were of the most horrible, as well as the most melancholy description. They came from the ranges of pallet-beds, which were closely packed together in a species of military hospital, where a burning fever was the prevalent complaint. Many of the patients were under the influence of a high delirium, during which they shouted, shrieked, laughed, blasphemed, and uttered the most horrible imprecations. Others, sensible of their condition, bewailed it with low groans, and some attempts at devotion, which showed their ignorance of the principles, and even the forms of religion. Those who were convalescent talked ribaldry in a loud tone, or whispered to each other in cant language, upon schemes which, as far as a passing phrase could be understood by a novice, had relation to violent and criminal exploits.

Richard Middlemas's astonishment was equal to his horror. He had but one advantage over the poor wretches with whom he was classed, and it was in enjoying the luxury of a pallet to himself—most of the others being occupied by two unhappy beings. He saw no one who appeared to attend to the wants, or to heed the complaints, of the wretches around him, or to whom he could offer any appeal against his present situation. He looked for his clothes, that he might arise and extricate himself from this den of horrors; but his clothes were nowhere to be seen, nor did he see his portmanteau, or sea-chest. It was much to be apprehended he would never see them more.

Then, but too late, he remembered the insinuations which had passed current respecting his friend the Captain, who was supposed to have been discharged by Mr. Lawford, on account of some breach of trust in the Town-Clerk's service. But that he should have trepanned the friend who had reposed his whole confidence in him—that he should have plundered him of his fortune, and placed him in this house of pestilence, with the hope that death might stifle his tongue—were iniquities not to have been, anticipated, even if the worst of these reports were true.

But Middlemas resolved not to be awanting to himself. This place must be visited by some officer, military or medical, to whom he would make an appeal, and alarm his fears at least, if he could not awaken his conscience. While he revolved these distracting thoughts, tormented at the same time by a burning thirst which he had no means of satisfying, he endeavoured to discover if, amongst those stretched upon the pallets nearest him, he could not discern some one likely to enter into conversation with him, and give him some information about the nature and customs of this horrid place. But the bed nearest him was occupied by two fellows, who, although to judge from their gaunt cheeks, hollow eyes, and ghastly looks, they were apparently recovering from the disease, and just rescued from the jaws of death, were deeply engaged in endeavouring to cheat each other of a few half-pence at a game of cribbage, mixing the terms of the game with oaths not loud but deep; each turn of luck being hailed by the winner as well as the loser with execrations, which seemed designed to blight both body and soul, now used as the language of triumph, and now as reproaches against fortune.

Next to the gamblers was a pallet, occupied indeed by two bodies, but only one of which was living—the other sufferer had been recently relieved from his agony.

"He is dead—he is dead!" said the wretched survivor.

"Then do you die too, and be d—d," answered one of the players, "and then there will be a pair of you, as Pugg says."

"I tell you he is growing stiff and cold," said the poor wretch—"the dead is no bed-fellow for the living—For God's sake help to rid me of the corpse."

"Ay, and get the credit of having *done* him—as may be the case with, yourself, friend—for he had some two or three hoggs about him"—

"You know you took the last rap from his breeches-pocket not an hour ago," expostulated the poor convalescent—"But help me to take the body out of the bed, and I will not tell the *jigger-dubber* that you have been beforehand with him."

"You tell the *jigger-dubber!*" answered the cribbage player. "Such another word, and I will twist your head round till your eyes look at the drummer's handwriting on your back. Hold your peace, and don't bother our game with your gammon, or I will make you as mute as your bedfellow."

The unhappy wretch, exhausted, sunk back beside his hideous companion, and the usual jargon of the game, interlarded with execrations, went on as before.

From this specimen of the most obdurate indifference, contrasted with the last excess of misery, Middlemas became satisfied how little could be made of an appeal to the humanity of his fellow-sufferers. His heart sunk within him, and the thoughts of the happy and peaceful home, which he might have called his own, rose before his over-heated fancy, with a vividness of perception that bordered upon insanity. He saw before him the rivulet which wanders through the burgh-muir of Middlemas, where he had so often set little mills for the amusement of Menie while she was a child. One draught of it would have been worth all the diamonds of the East, which of late he had worshipped with such devotion; but that draught was denied to him as to Tantalus.

Rallying his senses from this passing illusion, and knowing enough of the practice of the medical art, to be aware of the necessity of preventing his ideas from wandering if possible, he endeavoured to recollect that he was a surgeon, and, after all, should not have the extreme fear for the interior of a military hospital, which its horrors might inspire into strangers to the profession. But though he strove, by such recollections, to rally his spirits, he was not the less aware of the difference betwixt the condition of a surgeon, who might have attended such a place in the course of his duty, and a poor inhabitant, who was at once a patient and a prisoner.

A footstep was now heard in the apartment, which seemed to silence all the varied sounds of woe that filled it. The cribbage party hid their cards, and ceased their oaths; other wretches, whose complaints had arisen to frenzy, left off their wild exclamations and entreaties for assistance. Agony softened her shriek, Insanity hushed its senseless clamours, and even Death seemed desirous to stifle his parting groan in the presence of Captain Seelencooper. This official was the superintendent, or, as the miserable inhabitants termed him, the Governor of the Hospital. He had all the air of having been originally a turnkey in some ill-regulated jail—a stout, short, bandy-legged man, with one eye, and a double portion of ferocity in that which remained. He wore an old-fashioned tarnished uniform, which did not seem to have been made for him; and the voice in which this minister of humanity addressed the sick, was that of a boatswain, shouting in the midst of a storm. He had pistols and a cutlass in his belt; for his mode of administration being such as provoked even hospital patients to revolt, his life had been more than once in danger amongst them. He was followed by two assistants, who carried hand-cuffs and strait-jackets.

As Seelencooper made his rounds, complaint and pain were hushed, and the flourish of the bamboo, which he bore in his hand, seemed powerful as the wand of a magician to silence all complaint and remonstrance.

"I tell you the meat is as sweet as a nosegay—and for the bread, it's good enough, and too good, for a set of lubbers, that lie shamming Abraham, and consuming the Right Honourable Company's victuals—I don't speak to them that are really sick, for God knows I am always for humanity."

"If that be the case, sir," said Richard Middlemas, whose lair the Captain had approached, while he was thus answering the low and humble complaints of those by whose bed-side he passed—"if that be the case, sir, I hope your humanity will make you attend to what I say."

"And—who the devil are you?" said the Governor, turning on him his single eye of fire, while a sneer gathered on his harsh features, which were so well qualified to express it.

"My name is Middlemas—I come from Scotland, and have been sent here by some strange mistake. I am neither a private soldier, nor am I indisposed, more than by the heat of this cursed place."

"Why then, friend, all I have to ask you is, whether you are an attested recruit or not?"

"I was attested at Edinburgh," said Middlemas, "but"—

"But what the devil would you have then?—you are enlisted—the Captain and the Doctor sent you here—surely they know best whether you are private or officer, sick or well."

"But I was promised," said Middlemas, "promised by Tom Hillary"—

"Promised, were you? Why, there is not a man here that has not been promised something by somebody or another, or perhaps has promised something to himself. This is the land of promise, my smart fellow, but you know it is India that must be the land of performance. So, good morning to you. The Doctor will come his rounds presently and put you all to rights."

"Stay but one moment—one moment only—I have been robbed."

"Robbed! look you there now," said the Governor—"everybody that comes here has been robbed.—Egad, I am the luckiest fellow in Europe—other people in my line have only thieves and blackguards upon their hands; but none come to my ken but honest, decent, unfortunate gentlemen, that have been robbed!"

"Take care how you treat this so lightly, sir," said Middlemas; "I have been robbed of a thousand pounds."

Here Governor Seelencooper's gravity was totally overcome, and his laugh was echoed by several of the patients, either because they wished to curry favour with the superintendent, or from the feeling which influences evil spirits to rejoice in the tortures of those who are sent to share their agony.

"A thousand pounds!" exclaimed Captain Seelencooper, as he recovered his breath,—"Come, that's a good one—I like a fellow that does not make two bites of a cherry—why, there is not a cull in the ken that pretends to have lost more than a few hoggs, and here is a servant to the Honourable Company that has been robbed of a thousand pounds! Well done, Mr. Tom of Ten Thousand-you're a credit to the house, and to the service, and so good morning to you."

He passed on, and Richard, starting up in a storm of anger and despair, found, as he would have called after him, that his voice, betwixt thirst and agitation, refused its office. "Water, water!" he said, laying hold, at the same time, of one of the assistants who followed Seelencooper by the sleeve. The fellow looked carelessly round; there was a jug stood by the side of the cribbage players, which he reached to Middlemas, bidding him, "Drink and be d—d."

The man's back was no sooner turned, than the gamester threw himself from his own bed into that of Middlemas, and grasping firm hold of the arm of Richard, ere he could carry the vessel to his head, swore he should not have his booze. It may be readily conjectured, that the pitcher thus anxiously and desperately reclaimed, contained something better than the pure element. In fact, a large proportion of it was gin. The jug was broken in the struggle, and the liquor spilt. Middlemas dealt a blow to the assailant, which was amply and heartily repaid, and a combat would have ensued, but for the interference of the superintendent and his assistants, who, with a dexterity that showed them well acquainted with such emergencies, clapped a straight-waistcoat upon each of the antagonists. Richard's efforts at remonstrance only procured him a blow from Captain Seelencooper's rattan, and a tender admonition to hold his tongue, if he valued a whole skin.

Irritated at once by sufferings of the mind and of the body, tormented by raging thirst, and by the sense of his own dreadful situation, the mind of Richard Middlemas seemed to be on the point of becoming unsettled. He felt an insane desire to imitate and reply to the groans, oaths, and ribaldry, which, as soon as the superintendent quitted the hospital, echoed around him. He longed, though he struggled against the impulse, to vie in curses with the reprobate, and in screams with the maniac. But his tongue clove to the roof of his mouth, his mouth itself seemed choked with ashes; there came upon him a dimness of sight, a rushing sound in his ears, and the powers of life were for a time suspended.

CHAPTER 7

A wise physician, skill'd our wounds to heal,
Is more than armies to the common weal.

POPE'S Homer.

As Middlemas returned to his senses, he was sensible that his blood felt more cool; that the feverish throb of his pulsation was diminished; that the ligatures on his person were removed, and his lungs performed their functions more freely. One assistant was binding up a vein, from which a considerable quantity of blood had been taken; another, who had just washed the face of the patient, was holding aromatic vinegar to his nostrils. As he began to open his eyes, the person who had just completed the bandage, said in Latin, but in a very low tone, and without raising his head, "Annon sis Ricardus ille Middlemas, ex civitate Middlemassiense? Responde in lingua Latina."

"Sum ille miserrimus," replied Richard, again shutting his eyes; for, strange as it may seem, the voice of his comrade Adam Hartley, though his presence might be of so much consequence in this emergency, conveyed a pang to his wounded pride. He was conscious of unkindly, if not hostile, feelings towards his old companion; he remembered the tone of superiority which he used to assume over him, and thus to lie stretched at his feet, and in a manner at his mercy, aggravated his distress, by the feelings of the dying chieftain, "Earl Percy sees my fall." This was, however, too unreasonable an emotion to subsist above a minute. In the next, he availed himself of the Latin language, with which both were familiar, (for in that time the medical studies at the celebrated University of Edinburgh were, in a great measure, conducted in Latin,) to tell in a few words his own folly, and the villany of Hillary.

"I must be gone instantly," said Hartley—"Take courage—I trust to be able to assist you. In the meantime, take food and physic from none but my servant, who you see holds the sponge in his hand. You are in a place where a man's life has been taken for the sake of his gold sleeve-buttons."

"Stay yet a moment," said Middlemas—"Let me remove this temptation from my dangerous neighbours."

He drew a small packet from his under waistcoat, and put it into Hartley's hands.

"If I die," he said, "be my heir. You deserve her better than I."

All answer was prevented by the hoarse voice of Seelencooper.

"Well, Doctor, will you carry through your patient?"

"Symptoms are dubious yet," said the Doctor—"That was an alarming swoon. You must have him carried into the private ward, and my young man shall attend him.

"Why, if you command it, Doctor, needs must;—but I can tell you there is a man we both know, that has a thousand reasons at least for keeping him in the public ward."

"I know nothing of your thousand reasons," said Hartley; "I can only tell you that this young fellow is as well-limbed and likely a lad as the Company have among their recruits. It is my business to save him for their service, and if he dies by your neglecting what I direct, depend upon it I will not allow the blame to lie at my door. I will tell the General the charge I have given you."

"The General!" said Seelencooper, much embarrassed—"Tell the General?—ay, about his health. But you will not say any thing about what he may have said in his light-headed fits? My eyes! if you listen to what feverish patients say when the tantivy is in their brain, your back will soon break with tale-bearing, for I will warrant you plenty of them to carry."

"Captain Seelencooper," said the Doctor, "I do not meddle with your department in the hospital; my advice to you is, not to trouble yourself with mine. I suppose, as I have a commission in the service, and have besides a regular diploma as a physician, I know when my patient is light-headed or otherwise. So do you let the man be carefully looked after, at your peril."

Thus saying, he left the hospital, but not till, under pretext of again consulting the pulse, he pressed the patient's hand, as if to assure him once more of his exertions for his liberation.

"My eyes!" muttered Seelencooper, "this cockerel crows gallant, to come from a Scotch roost; but I would know well enough how to fetch the youngster off the perch, if it were not for the cure he has done on the General's pickaninies."

Enough of this fell on Richard's ear to suggest hopes of deliverance, which were increased when he was shortly afterwards removed to a separate ward, a place much more decent in appearance, and inhabited only by two patients, who seemed petty officers. Although sensible that he had no illness, save that weakness which succeeds violent agitation, he deemed it wisest to suffer himself still to be treated as a patient, in consideration that he should thus remain under his comrade's superintendence. Yet while preparing to avail himself of Hartley's good offices, the prevailing reflection of his secret bosom was the ungrateful sentiment, "Had Heaven no other means of saving me than by the hands of him I like least on the face of the earth?"

Meanwhile, ignorant of the ungrateful sentiments of his comrade, and indeed wholly indifferent how he felt towards him, Hartley proceeded in doing him such service as was in his power, without any other object than the discharge of his own duty as a man and as a Christian. The manner in which he became qualified to render his comrade assistance, requires some short explanation.

Our story took place at a period, when the Directors of the East India Company, with that hardy and persevering policy which has raised to such a height the British Empire in the East, had determined to send a large re-inforcement of European troops to the support of their power in India, then threatened by the kingdom of Mysore, of which the celebrated Hyder Ali had usurped the government, after dethroning his master. Considerable difficulty was found in obtaining recruits for that service. Those who might have been otherwise disposed to be soldiers, were afraid of the climate, and of the spe-cies of banishment which the engagement implied; and doubted also how far the engagements of the Company might be faithfully observed towards them, when they were removed from the protection of the British laws. For these and other reasons, the military service of the King was preferred, and that of the Company could only procure the worst recruits, although their zealous agents scrupled not to employ the worst means. Indeed the practice of kidnapping, or crimping, as it is technically called, was at that time gen-eral, whether for the colonies, or even for the King's troops; and as the agents employed in such transactions must be of course entirely unscrupulous, there was not only much villany committed in the direct prosecution of the trade, but it gave rise incidentally to remarkable cases of robbery, and even murder. Such atrocities were of course concealed from the authorities for whom the levies were made, and the necessity of obtaining soldiers made men, whose conduct was otherwise unexceptionable, cold in looking closely into the mode in which their recruiting service was conducted.

The principal depot of the troops which were by these means assembled, was in the Isle of Wight, where the season proving unhealthy, and the men themselves being many of them of a bad habit of body, a fever of a malignant character broke out amongst them, and speedily crowded with patients the military hospital, of which Mr. Seelencooper, himself an old and experienced crimp and kidnapper, had obtained the superintendence. Irregularities began to take place also among the soldiers who remained healthy, and the neces-sity of subjecting them to some discipline before they sailed was so evident, that several officers of the Company's naval service expressed their belief that otherwise there would be dangerous mutinies on the passage.

To remedy the first of these evils, the Court of Directors sent down to the island several of their medical servants, amongst whom was Hartley, whose qualifications had been amply certified by a medical board, before which he had passed an examination, besides his possessing a diploma from the University of Edinburgh as M. D.

To enforce the discipline of their soldiers, the Court committed full power to one of their own body, General Witherington. The General was an officer who had distinguished himself highly in their service. He had returned from India five or six years before, with a large fortune, which he had rendered much greater by an advantageous marriage with a rich heiress. The General and his lady went little into society, but seemed to live entirely for their infant family, those in number being three, two boys and a girl. Although he had retired from the service, he willingly undertook the temporary charge committed to him, and taking a house at a considerable distance from the town of Ryde, he proceeded to enrol the troops into separate bodies, appoint officers of capacity to each, and by regular training and discipline, gradually to bring them into something resembling good order. He heard their complaints of ill usage in the articles of provisions and appointments, and did them upon all occasions the strictest justice, save that he was never known to restore one recruit to his freedom from the service, however unfairly or even illegally his attestation might have been obtained.

"It is none of my business," said General Witherington, "how you became soldiers,—soldiers I found you, and soldiers I will leave you. But I will take especial care, that as soldiers you shall have every thing, to a penny or a pin's head, that you are justly entitled to." He went to work without fear or favour, reported many abuses to the Board of Directors, had several officers, commissaries, &c. removed from the service, and made his name as great a terror to the peculators at home, as it had been to the enemies of Britain in Hindostan.

Captain Seelencooper, and his associates in the hospital department, heard and trembled, fearing that their turn should come next; but the General, who elsewhere examined all with his own eyes, showed a reluctance to visit the hospital in person. Public report industriously imputed this to fear of infection. Such was certainly the motive; though it was not fear for his own safety that influenced General Witherington, but he dreaded lest he should carry the infection home to the nursery, on which he doated. The alarm of his lady was yet more unreasonably sensitive: she would scarcely suffer the children to walk abroad, if the wind but blew from the quarter where the hospital was situated.

But Providence baffles the precautions of mortals. In a walk across the fields, chosen as the most sheltered and sequestered, the children, with their train of Eastern and European attendants, met a woman who carried a child that was recovering from the small-pox. The anxiety of the father, joined to some religious scruples on the mother's part, had postponed inoculation, which was then scarcely come into general use. The infection caught like a quick-match, and ran like wildfire through all those in the family who had not previously had the disease. One of the General's children, the second boy, died, and two of the Ayas, or black female servants, had the same fate. The hearts of the father and mother would have been broken for the child they had lost, had not their grief been suspended by anxiety for the fate of those who lived, and who were confessed to be in imminent danger. They were like persons distracted, as the symptoms of the poor patients appeared gradually to resemble more nearly that of the child already lost.

While the parents were in this agony of apprehension, the General's principal servant, a native of Northumberland like himself, informed him one morning that there was a young man from the same county among the hospital doctors, who had publicly blamed the mode of treatment observed towards the patients, and spoken of another which he had seen practised with eminent success.

"Some impudent quack," said the General, "who would force himself into business by bold assertions. Doctor Tourniquet and Doctor Lancelot are men of high reputation."

"Do not mention their reputation," said the mother, with a mother's impatience, "did they not let my sweet Reuben die? What avails the reputation of the physician, when the patient perisheth?"

"If his honour would but see Doctor Hartley," said Winter, turning half towards the lady, then turning back again to his master. "He is a very decent young man, who, I am sure, never expected what he said to reach your honour's ears;—and he is a native of Northumberland."

"Send a servant with a led horse," said the General; "let the young man come hither instantly."

It is well known, that the ancient mode of treating the small-pox was to refuse to the patient every thing which Nature urged him to desire; and, in particular, to confine him to heated rooms, beds loaded with blankets, and spiced wine, when Nature called for cold water and fresh air. A different mode of treatment had of late been adventured upon by some practitioners, who preferred reason to authority, and Gideon Gray had followed it for several years with extraordinary success.

When General Witherington saw Hartley, he was startled at his youth; but when he heard him modestly, but with confidence, state the difference of the two modes of treatment, and the rationale of his practice, he listened with the most serious attention. So did his lady, her streaming eyes turning from Hartley to her husband, as if to watch what impression the arguments of the former were making upon the latter. General Witherington was silent for a few minutes after Hartley had finished his exposition, and seemed buried in profound reflection. "To treat a fever," he said, "in a manner which tends to produce one, seems indeed to be adding fuel to fire."

"It is—it is," said the lady. "Let us trust this young man, General Witherington. We shall at least give our darlings the comforts of the fresh air and cold water, for which they are pining."

But the General remained undecided. "Your reasoning," he said to Hartley, "seems plausible; but still it is only hypothesis. What can you show to support your theory, in opposition to the general practice?"

"My own observation," replied the young man. "Here is a memorandum-book of medical cases which I have witnessed. It contains twenty cases of small-pox, of which eighteen were recoveries."

"And the two others?" said the General.

"Terminated fatally," replied Hartley; "we can as yet but partially disarm this scourge of the human race."

"Young man," continued the General, "were I to say that a thousand gold mohrs were yours in case my children live under your treatment, what have you to peril in exchange?"

"My reputation," answered Hartley, firmly.

"And you could warrant on your reputation the recovery of your patients?"

"God forbid I should be presumptuous! But I think I could warrant my using those means, which, with God's blessing, afford the fairest chance of a favourable result."

"Enough—you are modest and sensible, as well as bold, and I will trust you."

The lady, on whom Hartley's words and manner had made a great impression, and who was eager to discontinue a mode of treatment which subjected the patients to the greatest pain and privation, and had already proved unfortunate, eagerly acquiesced, and Hartley was placed in full authority in the sick room.

Windows were thrown open, fires reduced or discontinued, loads of bed-clothes removed, cooling drinks superseded mulled wine and spices. The sick-nurses cried out murder. Doctors Tourniquet and Lancelot retired in disgust, menacing something like a general pestilence, in vengeance of what they termed rebellion against the neglect of the aphorisms of Hippocrates. Hartley proceeded quietly and steadily, and the patients got into a fair road of recovery.

The young Northumbrian was neither conceited nor artful; yet, with all his plainness of character, he could not but know the influence which a successful physician obtains over the parents of the children whom he has saved from the grave, and especially before the cure is actually completed. He resolved to use this influence in behalf of his old companion, trusting that the military tenacity of General Witherington would give way on consideration of the obligation so lately conferred upon him.

On his way to the General's house, which was at present his constant place of residence, he examined the package which Middlemas had put into his hand. It contained the picture of Menie Gray, plainly set, and the ring, with brilliants, which Doctor Gray had given to Richard, as his mother's last gift. The first of these tokens extracted from honest Hartley a sigh, perhaps a tear of sad remembrance. "I fear," he said, "she has not chosen worthily; but she shall be happy, if I can make her so."

Arrived at the residence of General Witherington, our Doctor went first to the sick apartment, and then carried to their parents the delightful account, that the recovery of the children might be considered as certain.

"May the God of Israel bless thee, young man!" said the lady, trembling with emotion; "thou hast wiped the tear from the eye of the despairing mother. And yet—alas! alas! still it must flow when I think of my cherub Reuben.—Oh! Mr. Hartley, why did we not know you a week sooner!—my darling had not then died."

"God gives and takes away, my lady," answered Hartley; "and you must remember that two are restored to you out of three. It is far from certain, that the treatment I have used towards the convalescents would have brought through their brother; for the case, as reported to me, waa of a very inveterate description."

"Doctor," said Witherington, his voice testifying more emotion than he usually or willingly gave way to, "you can comfort the sick in spirit as well as the sick in body. But it is time we settle our wager. You betted your reputation, which remains with you, increased by all the credit due to your eminent success, against a thousand gold mohrs, the value of which you will find in that pocketbook."

"General Witherington," said Hartley, "you are wealthy, and entitled to be generous—I am poor, and not entitled to decline whatever may be, even in a liberal sense, a compensation for my professional attendance. But there is a bound to extravagance, both in giving and accepting; and I must not hazard the newly acquired reputation with which you flatter me, by giving room to have it said, that I fleeced the parents, when their feelings were all afloat with anxiety for their children.—Allow me to divide this large sum; one half I will thankfully retain, as a most liberal recompense for my labour; and if you still think you owe me any thing, let me have it in the advantage of your good opinion and countenance."

"If I acquiesce in your proposal, Doctor Hartley," said the General, reluctantly receiving back a part of the contents of the pocketbook, "it is because I hope to serve you with my interest, even better than with my purse."

"And indeed, sir," replied Hartley, "it was upon your interest that I am just about to make a small claim."

The General and his lady spoke both in the same breath, to assure him his boon was granted before asked.

"I am not so sure of that," said Hartley; "for it respects a point on which I have heard say, that your Excellency is rather inflexible—the discharge of a recruit."

"My duty makes me so," replied the General—"You know the sort of fellows that we are obliged to content ourselves with—they get drunk—grow pot-valiant—enlist over-night, and repent next morning. If I am to dismiss all those who pretend to have been trepanned, we should have few volunteers remain behind. Every one has some idle story of the promises of a swaggering sergeant Kite—It is impossible to attend to them. But let me hear yours, however."

"Mine is a very singular case. The party has been robbed of a thousand pounds."

"A recruit for this service possessing a thousand pounds! My dear Doctor, depend upon it, the fellow has gulled you. Bless my heart, would a man who had a thousand pounds think of enlisting as a private sentinel?"

"He had no such thoughts," answered Hartley. "He was persuaded by the rogue whom he trusted, that he was to have a commission."

"Then his friend must have been Tom Hillary, or the devil; for no other could possess so much cunning and impudence. He will certainly find his way to the gallows at last. Still this story of the thousand pounds seems a touch even beyond Tom Hillary. What reason have you to think that this fellow ever had such a sum of money?"

"I have the best reason to know it for certain," answered Hartley; "he and I served our time together, under the same excellent master; and when he came of age, not liking the profession which he had studied, and obtaining possession of his little fortune, he was deceived by the promises of this same Hillary."

"Who has had him locked up in our well-ordered hospital yonder?" said the General.

"Even so, please your Excellency," replied Hartley; "not, I think, to cure him of any complaint, but to give him the opportunity of catching one, which would silence all enquiries."

"The matter shall be closely looked into. But how miserably careless the young man's friends must have been to let a raw lad go into the world with such a companion and guide as Tom Hillary, and such a sum as a thousand pounds in his pocket. His parents had better have knocked him on the head. It certainly was not done like canny Northumberland, as my servant Winter calls it."

"The youth must indeed have had strangely hard-hearted, or careless parents," said Mrs. Witherington, in accents of pity.

"He never knew them, madam," said Hartley; "there was a mystery on the score of his birth. A cold, unwilling, and almost unknown hand, dealt him out his portion when he came of lawful age, and he was pushed into the world like a bark forced from shore, without rudder, compass, or pilot."

Here General Witherington involuntarily looked to his lady, while, guided by a similar impulse, her looks were turned upon him. They exchanged a momentary glance of deep and peculiar meaning, and then the eyes of both were fixed on the ground.

"Were you brought up in Scotland?" said the lady, addressing herself, in a faltering voice, to Hartley—"And what was your master's name?"

"I served my apprenticeship with Mr. Gideon Gray of the town of Middlemas," said Hartley.

"Middlemas! Gray?" repeated the lady, and fainted away.

Hartley offered the succours of his profession; the husband flew to support her head, and the instant that Mrs. Witherington began to recover, he whispered to her, in a tone betwixt entreaty and warning, "Zilia, beware—beware!"

Some imperfect sounds which she had begun to frame, died away upon her tongue.

"Let me assist you to your dressing-room, my love," said her obviously anxious husband.

She arose with the action of an automaton, which moves at a touch of a spring, and half hanging upon her husband, half dragging herself on by her own efforts, had nearly reached the door of the room, when Hartley following, asked if he could be of any service.

"No, sir," said the General, sternly; "this is no case for a stranger's interference; when you are wanted I will send for you."

Hartley stepped back on receiving a rebuff in a tone so different from that which General Witherington had used towards him in their previous intercourse, and felt disposed for the first time, to give credit to public report, which assigned to that gentleman, with several good qualities, the character of a very proud and haughty man. Hitherto, he thought, I have seen him tamed by sorrow and anxiety, now the mind is regaining its natural tension. But he must in decency interest himself for this unhappy Middlemas.

The General returned into the apartment a minute or two afterwards, and addressed Hartley in his usual tone of politeness, though apparently still under great embarrassment, which he in vain endeavoured to conceal.

"Mrs. Witherington is better," he said, "and will be glad to see you before dinner. You dine with us, I hope?"

Hartley bowed.

"Mrs. Witherington is rather subject to this sort of nervous fits, and she has been much harassed of late by grief and apprehension. When she recovers from them it is a few minutes before she can collect her ideas, and during such intervals—to speak very confidentially to you, my dear Doctor Hartley—she speaks sometimes about imaginary events which have never happened, and sometimes about distressing occurrences in an early period of life. I am not, therefore, willing that any one but myself, or her old attendant Mrs. Lopez, should be with her on such occasions."

Hartley admitted that a certain degree of light-headedness was often the consequence of nervous fits.

The General proceeded. "As to this young man—this friend of yours—this Richard Middlemas—did you not call him so?"

"Not that I recollect," answered Hartley; "but your Excellency has hit upon his name."

"That is odd enough—Certainly you said something about Middlemas?" replied General Witherington.

"I mentioned the name of the town," said Hartley.

"Ay, and I caught it up as the name of the recruit—I was indeed occupied at the moment by my anxiety about my wife. But this Middlemas, since such is his name, is a wild young fellow, I suppose?"

"I should do him wrong to say so, your Excellency. He may have had his follies like other young men; but his conduct has, so far as I know, been respectable; but, considering we lived in the same house, we were not very intimate."

"That is bad—I should have liked him—that is—it would have been happy for him to have had a friend like you. But I suppose you studied too hard for him. He would be a soldier, ha?—Is he good-looking?"

"Remarkably so," replied Hartley; "and has a very prepossessing manner."

"Is his complexion dark or fair?" asked the General.

"Rather uncommonly dark," said Hartley,—"darker, if I may use the freedom, than your Excellency's."

"Nay, then, he must be a black ouzel, indeed!—Does he understand languages?"

"Latin and French tolerably well."

"Of course he cannot fence or dance?"

"Pardon me, sir, I am no great judge; but Richard is reckoned to do both with uncommon skill."

"Indeed!—Sum this up, and it sounds well. Handsome, accomplished in exercises, moderately learned, perfectly well-bred, not unreasonably wild. All this comes too high for the situation of a private sentinel. He must have a commission, Doctor—entirely for your sake."

"Your Excellency is generous."

"It shall be so; and I will find means to make Tom Hillary disgorge his plunder, unless he prefers being hanged, a fate he has long deserved. You cannot go back to the Hospital to-day. You dine with us, and you know Mrs. Witherington's fears of infection; but to-morrow find out your friend. Winter shall see him equipped with every thing needful. Tom Hillary shall repay advances, you know; and he must be off with the first detachment of the recruits, in the Middlesex Indiaman, which sails from the Downs on Monday fortnight; that is, if you think him fit for the voyage. I dare say the poor fellow is sick of the Isle of Wight."

"Your Excellency will permit the young man to pay his respects to you before his departure?"

"To what purpose, sir?" said the General hastily and peremptorily; but instantly added, "You are right—I should like to see him. Winter shall let him know the time, and take horses to fetch him hither. But he must have been out of the Hospital for a day or two; so the sooner you can set him at liberty the better. In the meantime, take him to your own lodgings, Doctor; and do not let him form any intimacies with the officers, or any others, in this place, where he may light on another Hillary."

Had Hartley been as well acquainted as the reader with the circumstances of young Middlemas's birth, he might have drawn decisive conclusions from the behaviour of General Witherington, while his comrade was the topic of conversation. But as Mr. Gray and Middlemas himself were both silent on the subject, he knew little of it but from general report, which his curiosity had never induced him to scrutinize minutely. Nevertheless, what he did apprehend interested him so much, that he resolved upon trying a little experiment, in which he thought there could be no great harm. He placed on his finger the remarkable ring intrusted to his care by Richard Middlemas, and endeavoured to make it conspicuous in approaching Mrs. Witherington; taking care, however, that this occurred during her husband's absence. Her eyes had no sooner caught a sight of the gem, than they became riveted to it, and she begged a nearer sight of it, as strongly resembling one which she had given to a friend. Taking the ring from his finger, and placing it in her emaciated hand, Hartley informed her it was the property of the friend in whom he had just been endeavouring to interest the General. Mrs. Witherington retired in great emotion, but next day summoned Hartley to a private interview, the particulars of which, so far as are necessary to be known, shall be afterwards related.

On the succeeding day after these important discoveries, Middlemas, to his great delight, was rescued from his seclusion in the Hospital, and transferred to his comrade's lodgings in the town of Ryde, of which Hartley himself was a rare inmate; the anxiety of Mrs. Witherington detaining him at the General's house, long after his medical attendance might have been dispensed with.

Within two or three days a commission arrived for Richard Middlemas, as a lieutenant in the service of the East India Company. Winter, by his master's orders, put the wardrobe of the young officer on a suitable footing; while

Middlemas, enchanted at finding himself at once emancipated from his late dreadful difficulties, and placed under the protection of a man of such importance as the General, obeyed implicitly the hints transmitted to him by Hartley, and enforced by Winter, and abstained from going into public, or forming acquaintances with any one. Even Hartley himself he saw seldom; and, deep as were his obligations, he did not perhaps greatly regret the absence of one whose presence always affected him with a sense of humiliation and abasement.

CHAPTER 8

The evening before he was to sail for the Downs, where the Middlesex lay ready to weigh anchor, the new lieutenant was summoned by Winter to attend him to the General's residence, for the purpose of being introduced to his patron, to thank him at once, and to bid him farewell. On the road, the old man took the liberty of schooling his companion concerning the respect which he ought to pay to his master, "who was, though a kind and generous man as ever came from Northumberland, extremely rigid in punctiliously exacting the degree of honour which was his due."

While they were advancing towards the house, the General and his wife expected their arrival with breathless anxiety. They were seated in a superb drawing-room, the General behind a large chandelier, which, shaded opposite to his face, threw all the light to the other side of the table, so that he could observe any person placed there, without becoming the subject of observation in turn. On a heap of cushions, wrapped in a glittering drapery of gold and silver muslins, mingled with shawls, a luxury which was then a novelty in Europe, sate, or rather reclined, his lady, who, past the full meridian of beauty, retained charms enough to distinguish her as one who had been formerly a very fine woman, though her mind seemed occupied by the deepest emotion.

"Zilia," said her husband, "you are unable for what you have undertaken—take my advice—retire—you shall know all and everything that passes—but retire. To what purpose should you cling to the idle wish of beholding for a moment a being whom you can never again look upon?"

"Alas," answered the lady, "and is not your declaration that I shall never see him more, a sufficient reason that I should wish to see him now—should wish to imprint on my memory the features and the form which I am never again to behold while we are in the body? Do not, my Richard, be more cruel than was my poor father, even when his wrath was in its bitterness. He let me look upon my infant, and its cherub face dwelt with me, and was my comfort among the years of unutterable sorrow in which my youth wore away."

"It is enough, Zilia—you have desired this boon—I have granted it—and, at whatever risk, my promise shall be kept. But think how much depends on this fatal secret—your rank and estimation in society—my honour interested that that estimation should remain uninjured. Zilia, the moment that the promulgation of such a secret gives prudes and scandalmongers a right to treat you with scorn, will be fraught with unutterable misery, perhaps with bloodshed and death, should a man dare to take up the rumour."

"You shall be obeyed, my husband," answered Zilia, "in all that the frailness of nature will permit. But oh, God of my fathers, of what clay hast thou fashioned us poor mortals, who dread so much the shame which follows sin, yet repent so little for the sin itself!" In a minute afterwards steps were heard—the door opened—Winter announced Lieutenant Middlemas, and the unconscious son stood before his parents.

Witherington started involuntarily up, but immediately constrained himself to assume the easy deportment with which a superior receives a dependent, and which, in his own case, was usually mingled with a certain degree of hauteur. The mother had less command of herself. She, too, sprung up, as if with the intention of throwing herself on the neck of her son, for whom she had travailed and sorrowed. But the warning glance of her husband arrested her as if by magic, and she remained standing, with her beautiful head and neck somewhat advanced, her hands clasped together, and extended forward in the attitude of motion, but motionless, nevertheless, as a marble statue, to which the sculptor has given all the appearance of life, but cannot impart its powers. So strange a gesture and posture might have excited the young officer's surprise; but the lady stood in the shade, and he was so intent in looking upon his patron, that he was scarce even conscious of Mrs. Witherington's presence.

"I am happy in this opportunity," said Middlemas, observing that the General did not speak, "to return my thanks to General Witherington, to whom they never can be sufficiently paid."

The sound of his voice, though uttering words so indifferent, seemed to dissolve the charm which kept his mother motionless. She sighed deeply, relaxed the rigidity of her posture, and sunk back on the cushions from which she had started up. Middlemas turned a look towards her at the sound of the sigh, and the rustling of her drapery. The General hastened to speak.

"My wife, Mr. Middlemas, has been unwell of late—your friend, Mr. Hartley, might mention it to you—an affection of the nerves."

Mr. Middlemas was, of course, sorry and concerned.

"We have had distress in our family, Mr. Middlemas, from the ultimate and heart-breaking consequences of which we have escaped by the skill of your friend, Mr. Hartley. We will be happy if it is in our power to repay a part of our obligations in service to his friend and protege, Mr. Middlemas."

"I am only acknowledged as *his* protege, then," *thought* Richard; but he *said*, "Every one must envy his friend in having had the distinguished good fortune to be of use to General Witherington and his family."

"You have received your commission, I presume. Have you any particular wish or desire respecting your destination?"

"No, may it please your Excellency," answered Middlemas. "I suppose Hartley would tell your Excellency my unhappy state—that I am an orphan, deserted by the parents who cast me on the wide world, an outcast about whom nobody knows or cares, except to desire that I should wander far enough, and live obscurely enough, not to disgrace them by their connexion with me."

Zilia wrung her hands as he spoke, and drew her muslin veil closely around her head as if to exclude the sounds which excited her mental agony.

"Mr. Hartley was not particularly communicative about your affairs," said the General; "nor do I wish to give you the pain of entering into them. What I desire to know is, if you are pleased with your destination to Madras?"

"Perfectly, please your Excellency—anywhere, so that there is no chance of meeting the villain Hillary."

"Oh! Hillary's services are too necessary in the purlieus of St. Giles's, the Lowlights of Newcastle, and such like places, where human carrion can be picked up, to be permitted to go to India. However, to show you the knave has some grace, there are the notes of which you were robbed. You will find them the very same paper which you lost, except a small sum which the rogue had spent, but which a friend has made up, in compassion for your sufferings." Richard Middlemas sunk on one knee, and kissed the hand which restored him to independence.

"Pshaw!" said the General, "you are a silly young man;" but he withdrew not his hand from his caresses. This was one of the occasions on which Dick Middlemas could be oratorical.

"O, my more than father," he said, "how much greater a debt do I owe to you than to the unnatural parents, who brought me into this world by their sin, and deserted me through their cruelty!"

Zilia, as she heard these cutting words, flung back her veil, raising it on both hands till it floated behind her like a mist, and then giving a faint groan, sunk down in a swoon. Pushing Middlemas from him with a hasty movement, General Witherington flew to his lady's assistance, and carried her in his arms, as if she had been a child, into the anteroom, where an old servant waited with the means of restoring suspended animation, which the unhappy husband too truly anticipated might be useful. These were hastily employed, and succeeded in calling the sufferer to life, but in a state of mental emotion that was dreadful.

Her mind was obviously impressed by the last words which her son had uttered.—"Did you hear him, Richard," she exclaimed, in accents terribly loud, considering the exhausted state of her strength—"Did you hear the words? It was Heaven speaking our condemnation by the voice of our own child. But do not fear, my Richard, do not weep! I will answer the thunder of Heaven with its own music."

She flew to a harpsichord which stood in the room, and, while the servant and master gazed on each other, as if doubting whether her senses were about to leave her entirely, she wandered over the keys, producing a wilderness of harmony, composed of passages recalled by memory, or combined by her own musical talent, until at length her voice and instrument united in one of those magnificent hymns in which her youth had praised her Maker, with voice and harp, like the Royal Hebrew who composed it. The tear ebbed insensibly from the eyes which she turned upwards—her vocal tones, combining with those of the instrument, rose to a pitch of brilliancy seldom attained by the most distinguished performers, and then sunk into a dying cadence, which fell, never again to rise,—for the songstress had died with her strain.

The horror of the distracted husband may be conceived, when all efforts to restore life proved totally ineffectual. Servants were despatched for medical men—Hartley, and every other who could be found. The General precipitated himself into the apartment they had so lately left, and in his haste ran, against Middlemas, who, at the sound of the music from the adjoining apartment, had naturally approached nearer to the door, and surprised and startled by the sort of clamour, hasty steps, and confused voices which ensued, had remained standing there, endeavouring to ascertain the cause of so much disorder.

The sight of the unfortunate young man wakened the General's stormy passions to frenzy. He seemed to recognise his son only as the cause of his wife's death. He seized him by the collar, and shook him violently as he dragged him into the chamber of mortality.

"Come hither," he said, "thou for whom a life of lowest obscurity was too mean a fate—come hither, and look on the parents whom thou hast so much envied—whom thou hast so often cursed. Look at that pale emaciated form, a figure of wax, rather than flesh and blood—that is thy mother—that is the un-happy Zilia Moncada, to whom thy birth was the source of shame and misery, and to whom thy ill-omened presence has now brought death itself. And be-hold me"—he pushed the lad from him, and stood up erect, looking wellnigh in gesture and figure the apostate spirit he described—"Behold me," he said; "see you not my hair streaming with sulphur, my brow scathed with lightning? I am the Arch-Fiend—I am the father whom you seek—I am the accursed Richard Tresham, the seducer of Zilia, and the father of her murderer!"

Hartley entered while this horrid scene was passing. All attention to the deceased, he instantly saw, would be thrown away; and understanding, partly from Winter, partly from the tenor of the General's frantic discourse, the nature of the disclosure which had occurred, he hastened to put an end, if possible, to the frightful and scandalous scene which had taken place. Aware how delicately the General felt on the subject of reputation, he assailed him with remonstrances on such conduct, in presence of so many witnesses. But the mind had ceased to answer to that once powerful keynote.

"I care not if the whole world hear my sin and my punishment," said Witherington. "It shall not be again said of me, that I fear shame more than I repent sin. I feared shame only for Zilia, and Zilia is dead!"

"But her memory, General—spare the memory of your wife, in which the character of your children is involved."

"I have no children!" said the desperate and violent man. "My Reuben is gone to Heaven, to prepare a lodging for the angel who has now escaped from the earth in a flood of harmony, which can only be equalled where she is gone. The other two cherubs will not survive their mother. I shall be, nay, I already feel myself, a childless man."

"Yet I am your son," replied Middlemas, in a tone sorrowful, but at the same time tinged with sullen resentment—"Your son by your wedded wife. Pale as she lies there, I call upon you both to acknowledge my rights, and all who are present to bear witness to them."

"Wretch!" exclaimed the maniac father, "canst thou think of thine own sordid rights in the midst of death and frenzy? My son?—thou art the fiend who has occasioned my wretchedness in this world, and who will share my eternal misery in the next. Hence from my sight, and my curse go with thee!"

His eyes fixed on the ground, his arms folded on his breast, the haughty and dogged spirit of Middlemas yet seemed to meditate reply. But Hartley, Winter, and other bystanders interfered, and forced him from the apartment. As they endeavoured to remonstrate with him, he twisted himself out of their grasp, ran to the stables, and seizing the first saddled horse that he found, out of many that had been in haste got ready to seek for assistance, he threw himself on its back, and rode furiously off. Hartley was about to mount and follow him; but Winter and the other domestics threw themselves around him, and implored him not to desert their unfortunate master, at a time when the influence which he had acquired over him might be the only restraint on the violence of his passions.

"He had a *coup de soleil* in India," whispered Winter, "and is capable of any thing in his fits. These cowards cannot control him, and I am old and feeble."

Satisfied that General Witherington was a greater object of compassion than Middlemas, whom besides he had no hope of overtaking, and who he believed was safe in his own keeping, however violent might be his present emotions, Hartley returned where the greater emergency demanded his immediate care.

He found the unfortunate General contending with the domestics, who endeavoured to prevent his making his way to the apartment where his children slept, and exclaiming furiously—"Rejoice, my treasures—rejoice!—He has fled, who would proclaim your father's crime, and your mother's dishonour!—He has fled, never to return, whose life has been the death of one parent, and the ruin of another!—Courage, my children, your father is with you—he will make his way to you through a hundred obstacles!"

The domestics, intimidated and undecided, were giving way to him, when Adam Hartley approached, and placing himself before the unhappy man, fixed his eye firmly on the General's, while he said in a low but stern voice—"Madman, would you kill your children?"

The General seemed staggered in his resolution, but still attempted to rush past him. But Hartley, seizing him by the collar of his coat on each side, "You are my prisoner," he said; "I command you to follow me."

"Ha! prisoner, and for high treason? Dog, thou hast met thy death!"

The distracted man drew a poniard from his bosom, and Hartley's strength and resolution might not perhaps have saved his life, had not Winter mastered the General's right hand, and contrived to disarm him.

"I am your prisoner, then," he said; "use me civilly—and let me see my wife and children."

"You shall see them to-morrow," said Hartley; "follow us instantly, and without the least resistance."

General Witherington followed like a child, with the air of one who is suffering for a cause in which he glories.

"I am not ashamed of my principles," he said—"I am willing to die for my king."

Without exciting his frenzy, by contradicting the fantastic idea which occupied his imagination, Hartley continued to maintain over his patient the ascendency he had acquired. He caused him to be led to his apartment, and beheld him suffer himself to be put to bed. Administering then a strong composing draught, and causing a servant to sleep in the room, he watched the unfortunate man till dawn of morning.

General Witherington awoke in his full senses, and apparently conscious of his real situation, which he testified by low groans, sobs, and tears. When Hartley drew near his bedside, he knew him perfectly, and said, "Do not fear me—the fit is over—leave me now, and see after yonder unfortunate. Let him leave Britain as soon as possible, and go where his fate calls him, and where we can never meet more. Winter knows my ways, and will take care of me."

Winter gave the same advice. "I can answer," he said, "for my master's security at present; but in Heaven's name, prevent his ever meeting again, with that obdurate young man!"

CHAPTER 9

"Well, then, the world's mine oyster,
Which I with sword will open.

MERRY WIVES OF WINDSOR.

When Adam Hartley arrived at his lodgings in the sweet little town of Ryde, his first enquiries were after his comrade. He had arrived last night late, man and horse all in a foam. He made no reply to any questions about supper or the like, but snatching a candle, ran up stairs into his apartment, and shut and double-locked the door. The servants only supposed, that, being something intoxicated, he had ridden hard, and was unwilling to expose himself.

Hartley went to the door of his chamber, not without some apprehensions; and after knocking and calling more than once, received at length the welcome return, "Who is there?"

On Hartley announcing himself, the door opened, and Middlemas appeared, well dressed, and with his hair arranged and powdered; although, from the appearance of the bed, it had not been slept in on the preceding night, and Richard's countenance, haggard and ghastly, seemed to bear witness to the same fact. It was, however, with an affectation of indifference that he spoke.

"I congratulate you on your improvement in worldly knowledge, Adam. It is just the time to desert the poor heir, and to stick by him that is in immediate possession of the wealth."

"I staid last night at General Witherington's," answered Hartley, "because he is extremely ill."

"Tell him to repent of his sins, then," said Richard. "Old Gray used to say, a doctor had as good a title to give ghostly advice as a parson. Do you remember Doctor Dulberry, the minister, calling him an interloper? Ha! Ha! Ha!"

"I am surprised at this style of language from one in your circumstances."

"Why, ay," said Middlemas, with a bitter smile—"it would be difficult to most men to keep up their spirits, after gaining and losing father, mother, and a good inheritance, all in the same day. But I had always a turn for philosophy."

"I really do not understand you, Mr. Middlemas."

"Why, I found my parents yesterday, did I not?" answered the young man. "My mother, as you know, had waited but that moment to die, and my father to become distracted; and I conclude both were contrived purposely to cheat me of my inheritance, as he has taken up such a prejudice against me."

"Inheritance?" repeated Hartley, bewildered by Richard's calmness, and half suspecting that the insanity of the father was hereditary in the family. "In Heaven's name, recollect yourself, and get rid of these hallucinations. What inheritance are you dreaming of?"

"That of my mother, to be sure, who must have inherited old Moncada's wealth—and to whom should it descend, save to her children?—I am the eldest of them—that fact cannot be denied."

"But consider, Richard—recollect yourself."

"I do," said Richard; "and what then?"

"Then you cannot but remember," said Hartley, "that unless there was a will in your favour, your birth prevents you from inheriting."

"You are mistaken, sir, I am legitimate.—Yonder sickly brats, whom you rescued from the grave, are not more legitimate than I am.—Yes! our parents could not allow the air of Heaven to breathe on them—me they committed to the winds and the waves—I am nevertheless their lawful child, as well as their puling offspring of advanced age and decayed health. I saw them, Adam—Winter showed the nursery to me while they were gathering courage to receive me in the drawing-room. There they lay, the children of predilection, the riches of the East expended that they might sleep soft and wake in magnificence. I, the eldest brother—the heir—I stood beside their bed in the borrowed dress which I had so lately exchanged for the rags of an hospital. Their couches breathed the richest perfumes, while I was reeking from a pest-house; and I—I repeat it—the heir, the produce of their earliest and best love, was thus treated. No wonder that my look was that of a basilisk."

"You speak as if you were possessed with an evil spirit," said Hartley; "or else you labour under a strange delusion."

"You think those only are legally married over whom a drowsy parson has read the ceremony from a dog's-eared prayer-book? It may be so in your English law—but Scotland makes Love himself the priest. A vow betwixt a fond couple, the blue heaven alone witnessing, will protect a confiding girl against the perjury of a fickle swain, as much as if a Dean had performed the rites in the loftiest cathedral in England. Nay, more; if the child of love be acknowledged by the father at the time when he is baptized—if he present the mother to strangers of respectability as his wife, the laws of Scotland will not allow him to retract the justice which has, in these actions, been done to the female whom he has wronged, or the offspring of their mutual love. This General Tresham, or Witherington, treated my unhappy mother as his wife before Gray and others, quartered her as such in the family of a respectable man, gave her the same name by which he himself chose to pass for the time. He presented me to the priest as his lawful offspring; and the law of Scotland, benevolent to the helpless child, will not allow him now to disown what he so formally admitted. I know my rights, and am determined to claim them."

"You do not then intend to go on board the Middlesex? Think a little— You will lose your voyage and your commission."

"I will save my birth-right," answered Middlemas. "When I thought of going to India, I knew not my parents, or how to make good the rights which I had through them. That riddle is solved. I am entitled to at least a third of Moncada's estate, which, by Winter's account, is considerable. But for you, and your mode of treating the small-pox, I should have had the whole. Little did I think, when old Gray was likely to have his wig pulled off, for putting out fires, throwing open windows, and exploding whisky and water, that the new system of treating the small-pox was to cost me so many thousand pounds."

"You are determined then," said Hartley, "on this wild course?"

"I know my rights, and am determined to make them available," answered the obstinate youth.

"Mr. Richard Middlemas, I am sorry for you."

"Mr. Adam Hartley, I beg to know why I am honoured by your sorrow."

"I pity you," answered Hartley, "both for the obstinacy of selfishness, which can think of wealth after the scene you saw last night, and for the idle vision which leads you to believe that you can obtain possession of it."

"Selfish!" cried Middlemas; "why, I am a dutiful son, labouring to clear the memory of a calumniated mother—And am I a visionary?—Why, it was to this hope that I awakened, when old Moncada's letter to Gray, devoting me to perpetual obscurity, first roused me to a sense of my situation, and dispelled the dreams of my childhood. Do you think that I would ever have submitted to the drudgery which I shared with you, but that, by doing so, I kept in view the only traces of these unnatural parents, by means of which I proposed to introduce myself to their notice, and, if necessary, enforce the rights of a legitimate child? The silence and death of Moncada broke my plans, and it was then only I reconciled myself to the thoughts of India."

"You were very young to have known so much of the Scottish law, at the time when we were first acquainted," said Hartley. "But I can guess your instructor."

"No less authority than Tom Hillary's," replied Middlemas. "His good counsel on that head is a reason why I do not now prosecute him to the gallows."

"I judged as much," replied Hartley; "for I heard him, before I left Middlemas, debating the point with Mr. Lawford; and I recollect perfectly, that he stated the law to be such as you now lay down."

"And what said Lawford in answer?" demanded Middlemas.

"He admitted," replied Hartley, "that in circumstances where the case was doubtful, such presumptions of legitimacy might be admitted. But he said they were liable to be controlled by positive and precise testimony, as, for instance, the evidence of the mother declaring the illegitimacy of the child."

"But there can exist none such in my case," said Middlemas hastily, and with marks of alarm.

"I will not deceive you, Mr. Middlemas, though I fear I cannot help giving you pain. I had yesterday a long conference with your mother, Mrs. Witherington, in which she acknowledged you as her son, but a son born before marriage. This express declaration will, therefore, put an end to the suppositions on which you ground your hopes. If you please, you may hear the contents of her declaration, which I have in her own handwriting."

"Confusion! is the cup to be for ever dashed from my lips?" muttered Richard; but recovering his composure, by exertion of the self-command, of which he possessed so large a portion, he desired Hartley to proceed with his communication. Hartley accordingly proceeded to inform him of the particulars preceding his birth, and those which followed after it; while Middlemas, seated on a sea-chest, listened with inimitable composure to a tale which went to root up the flourishing hopes of wealth which he had lately so fondly entertained.

Zilia Moncada was the only child of a Portuguese Jew of great wealth, who had come to London, in prosecution of his commerce. Among the few Christians who frequented his house, and occasionally his table, was Richard Tresham, a gentleman of a high Northumbrian family, deeply engaged in the service of Charles Edward during his short invasion, and though holding a commission in the Portuguese service, still an object of suspicion to the British government, on account of his well-known courage and Jacobitical principles. The high-bred elegance of this gentleman, together with his complete acquaintance with the Portuguese language and manners, had won the intimacy of old Moncada, and, alas! the heart of the inexperienced Zilia, who, beautiful as an angel, had as little knowledge of the world and it's wickedness as the lamb that is but a week old.

Tresham made his proposals to Moncada, perhaps in a manner which too evidently showed that he conceived the high-born Christian was degrading himself in asking an alliance with the wealthy Jew. Moncada rejected his proposals, forbade him his house, but could not prevent the lovers from meeting in private. Tresham made a dishonourable use of the opportunities which the poor Zilia so incautiously afforded, and the consequence was her ruin. The lover, however, had every purpose of righting the injury which he had inflicted, and, after various plans of secret marriage, which were rendered abortive by the difference of religion, and other circumstances, flight for Scotland was determined on. The hurry of the journey, the fear and anxiety to which Zilia was subjected, brought on her confinement several weeks before the usual time, so that they were compelled to accept of the assistance and accommodation offered by Mr. Gray. They had not been there many hours ere Tresham heard, by the medium of some sharp-sighted or keen-eared friend, that there were warrants out against him for treasonable practices. His correspondence with Charles Edward had become known to Moncada during the period of their friendship; he betrayed it in vengeance to the British cabinet, and warrants were issued, in which, at Moncada's request, his daughter's name was included. This might be of use, he apprehended, to enable him to separate his daughter from Tresham, should he find the fugitives actually married. How far he succeeded, the reader already knows, as well as the precautions which he took to prevent the living evidence of his child's frailty from being known to exist. His daughter he carried with him, and subjected her to severe restraint, which her own reflections rendered doubly bitter. It would have completed his revenge, had the author of Zilia's misfortunes been brought to the scaffold for his political offences. But Tresham skulked among his friends in the Highlands, and escaped until the affair blew over.

He afterwards entered into the East India Company's service, under his mother's name of Witherington, which concealed the Jacobite and rebel, until these terms were forgotten. His skill in military affairs soon raised him to riches and eminence. When he returned to Britain, his first enquiries were after the family of Moncada. His fame, his wealth, and the late conviction that his daughter never would marry any but him who had her first love, induced the old man to give that encouragement to General Witherington, which he had always denied to the poor and outlawed Major Tresham; and the lovers, after having been fourteen years separated, were at length united in wedlock.

General Witherington eagerly concurred in the earnest wish of his father-in-law, that every remembrance of former events should be buried, by leaving the fruit of the early and unhappy intrigue suitably provided for, but in a distant and obscure situation. Zilia thought far otherwise. Her heart longed, with a mother's longing, towards the object of her first maternal tenderness, but she dared not place herself in opposition at once to the will of her father, and the decision of her husband. The former, his religious prejudices much effaced by his long residence in England, had given consent that she should conform to the established religion of her husband and her country,—the latter, haughty as we have described him, made it his pride to introduce the beautiful convert among his high-born kindred. The discovery of her former frailty would have proved a blow to her respectability, which he dreaded like death; and it could not long remain a secret from his wife, that in consequence of a severe illness in India, even his reason became occasionally shaken by anything which violently agitated his feelings. She had, therefore, acquiesced in patience and silence in the course of policy which Moncada had devised, and which her husband anxiously and warmly approved. Yet her thoughts, even when their marriage was blessed with other offspring, anxiously reverted to the banished and outcast child, who had first been clasped to the maternal bosom.

All these feelings, "subdued and cherished long," were set afloat in full tide by the unexpected discovery of this son, redeemed from a lot of extreme misery, and placed before his mother's imagination in circumstances so disastrous.

It was in vain that her husband had assured her that he would secure the young man's prosperity, by his purse and his interest. She could not be satisfied, until she had herself done something to alleviate the doom of banishment to which her eldest-born was thus condemned. She was the more eager to do so, as she felt the extreme delicacy of her health, which was undermined by so many years of secret suffering.

Mrs. Witherington was, in conferring her maternal bounty, naturally led to employ the agency of Hartley, the companion of her son, and to whom, since the recovery of her younger children, she almost looked up as to a tutelar deity. She placed in his hands a sum of £2000, which she had at her own unchallenged disposal, with a request, uttered in the fondest and most affectionate terms, that it might be applied to the service of Richard Middlemas in the way Hartley should think most useful to him. She assured him of further support, as it should be needed; and a note to the following purport was also intrusted him, to be delivered when and where the prudence of Hartley should judge it proper to confide to him the secret of his birth.

"Oh, Benoni! Oh, child of my sorrow!" said this interesting document, "why should the eyes of thy unhappy mother be about to obtain permission to look on thee, since her arms were denied the right to fold thee to her bosom? May the God of Jews and of Gentiles watch over thee, and guard thee! May he remove, in his good time, the darkness which rolls between me and the beloved of my heart—the first fruit of my unhappy, nay, unhallowed affection. Do not—do not, my beloved!—think thyself a lonely exile, while thy mother's prayers arise for thee at sunrise and at sunset, to call down every blessing on thy head—to invoke every power in thy protection and defence. Seek not to see me—Oh, why must I say so!—But let me humble myself in the dust, since it is my own sin, my own folly, which I must blame!—but seek not to see or speak with me—it might be the death of both. Confide thy thoughts to the excellent Hartley, who hath been the guardian angel of us all—even as the tribes of Israel had each their guardian angel. What thou shalt wish, and he shall advise in thy behalf, shall be done, if in the power of a mother—And the love of a mother! Is it bounded by seas, or can deserts and distance measure its limits? Oh, child of my sorrow! Oh, Benoni! let thy spirit be with mine, as mine is with thee." Z. M.

All these arrangements being completed, the unfortunate lady next insisted with her husband that she should be permitted to see her son in that parting interview which terminated so fatally. Hartley, therefore, now discharged as her executor, the duty intrusted to him as her confidential agent.

"Surely," he thought, as, having finished his communication, he was about to leave the apartment, "surely the demons of Ambition and Avarice will unclose the talons which they have fixed upon this man, at a charm like this."

And indeed Richard's heart had been formed of the nether millstone, had he not been duly affected by these first and last tokens of his mother's affection. He leant his head upon a table, and his tears flowed plentifully. Hartley left him undisturbed for more than an hour, and on his return found him in nearly the same attitude in which he had left him.

"I regret to disturb you at this moment," he said, "but I have still a part of my duty to discharge. I must place in your possession the deposit which your mother made in my hands—and I must also remind you that time flies fast, and that you have scarce an hour or two to determine whether you will prosecute your Indian voyage, under the new view of circumstances which I have opened to you."

Middlemas took the bills which his mother had bequeathed him. As he raised his head, Hartley could observe that his face was stained with tears. Yet he counted over the money with mercantile accuracy; and though he assumed the pen for the purpose of writing a discharge with an air of inconsolable dejection, yet he drew it up in good set terms, like one who had his senses much at his command.

"And now," he said, in a mournful voice, "give me my mother's narrative."

Hartley almost started, and answered hastily, "You have the poor lady's letter, which was addressed to yourself—the narrative is addressed to me. It is my warrant for disposing of a large sum of money—it concerns the rights of third parties, and I cannot part with it."

"Surely, surely it were better to deliver it into my hands, were it but to weep over it," answered Middlemas. "My fortune, Hartley, has been very cruel. You see that my parents purposed to have made me their undoubted heir; yet their purpose was disappointed by accident. And now my mother comes with well-intended fondness, and while she means to advance my fortune, furnishes evidence to destroy it.—Come, come, Hartley—you must be conscious that my mother wrote those details entirely for my information. I am the rightful owner, and insist on having them."

"I am sorry I must insist on refusing your demand," answered Hartley, putting the papers in his pocket. "You ought to consider, that if this communication has destroyed the idle and groundless hopes which you have indulged in, it has, at the same time, more than trebled your capital; and that if there are some hundreds or thousands in the world richer than yourself, there are many millions not half so well provided. Set a brave spirit, then, against your fortune, and do not doubt your success in life."

His words seemed to sink into the gloomy mind of Middlemas. He stood silent for a moment, and then answered with a reluctant and insinuating voice,—

"My dear Hartley, we have long been companions—you can have neither pleasure nor interest in ruining my hopes—you may find some in forwarding them. Moncada's fortune will enable me to allow five thousand pounds to the friend who should aid me in my difficulties."

"Good morning to you, Mr. Middlemas," said Hartley, endeavouring to withdraw.

"One moment—one moment," said Middlemas, holding his friend by the button at the same time, "I meant to say ten thousand—and—and—marry whomsoever you like—I will not be your hindrance."

"You are a villain!" said Hartley, breaking from him, "and I always thought you so."

"And you," answered Middlemas, "are a fool, and I never thought yon better. Off he goes—Let him—the game has been played and lost—I must hedge my bets: India must be my back-play."

All was in readiness for his departure. A small vessel and a favouring gale conveyed him and several other military gentlemen to the Downs, where the Indiaman, which was to transport them from Europe, lay ready for their reception.

His first feelings were sufficiently disconsolate. But accustomed from his infancy to conceal his internal thoughts, he appeared in the course of a week the gayest and best bred passenger who ever dared the long and weary space betwixt Old England and her Indian possessions. At Madras, where the sociable feelings of the resident inhabitants give ready way to enthusiasm in behalf of any stranger of agreeable qualities, he experienced that warm hospitality which distinguishes the British character in the East.

Middlemas was well received in company, and in the way of becoming an indispensable guest at every entertainment in the place, when the vessel, on board of which Hartley acted as surgeon's mate, arrived at the same settlement. The latter would not, from his situation, have been entitled to expect much civility and attention; but this disadvantage was made up by his possessing the most powerful introductions from General Withering-ton, and from other persons of weight in Leadenhall Street, the General's friends, to the principal inhabitants in the settlement. He found himself once more, therefore, moving in the same sphere with Middlemas, and under the alternative of living with him on decent and distant terms, or of breaking off with him altogether.

The first of these courses might perhaps have been the wisest; but the other was most congenial to the blunt and plain character of Hartley, who saw neither propriety nor comfort in maintaining a show of friendly intercourse, to conceal hate, contempt, and mutual dislike.

The circle at Fort St. George was much more restricted at that time than it has been since. The coldness of the young men did not escape notice; it transpired that they had been once intimates and fellow-students; yet it was now found that they hesitated at accepting invitations to the same parties. Rumour assigned many different and incompatible reasons for this deadly breach, to which Hartley gave no attention whatever, while Lieutenant Middlemas took care to countenance those which represented the cause of the quarrel most favourably to himself.

"A little bit of rivalry had taken place," he said, when pressed by gentlemen for an explanation; "he had only had the good luck to get further in the good graces of a fair lady than his friend Hartley, who had made a quarrel of it, as they saw. He thought it very silly to keep up spleen, at such a distance of time and space. He was sorry, more for the sake of the strangeness of the appearance of the thing than any thing else, although his friend had really some very good points about him."

While these whispers were working their effect in society, they did not prevent Hartley from receiving the most flattering assurances of encouragement and official promotion from the Madras government as opportunity should arise. Soon after, it was intimated to him that a medical appointment of a lucrative nature in a remote settlement was conferred on him, which removed him for some time from Madras and its neighbourhood.

Hartley accordingly sailed on his distant expedition; and it was observed, that after his departure, the character of Middlemas, as if some check had been removed, began to display itself in disagreeable colours. It was noticed that this young man, whose manners were so agreeable and so courteous during the first months after his arrival in India, began now to show symptoms of a haughty and overbearing spirit. He had adopted, for reasons which the reader may conjecture, but which appeared to be mere whim, at Fort St. George, the name of Tresham, in addition to that by which he had hitherto been distinguished, and in this he presisted with an obstinacy, which belonged more to the pride than the craft of his character. The Lieutenant-Colonel of the regiment, an old cross-tempered martinet, did not choose to indulge the Captain (such was now the rank of Middlemas) in this humour.

"He knew no officer," he said, "by any name save that which he bore in his commission," and he Middlemass'd the Captain on all occasions.

One fatal evening, the Captain was so much provoked, as to intimate peremptorily, "that he knew his own name best."

"Why, Captain Middlemas," replied the Colonel, "it is not every child that knows its own father, so how can every man be so sure of his own name?"

The bow was drawn at a venture, but the shaft found the rent in the armour, and stung deeply. In spite of all the interposition which could be attempted, Middlemas insisted on challenging the Colonel, who could be persuaded to no apology.

"If Captain Middlemas," he said, "thought the cap fitted, he was welcome to wear it."

The result was a meeting, in which, after the parties had exchanged shots, the seconds tendered their mediation. It was rejected by Middlemas, who, at the second fire, had the misfortune to kill his commanding officer. In consequence, he was obliged to fly from the British settlements; for, being universally blamed for having pushed the quarrel to extremity, there was little doubt that the whole severity of military discipline would be exercised upon the delinquent. Middlemas, therefore, vanished from Fort St. George, and, though the affair had made much noise at the time, was soon no longer talked of. It was understood, in general, that he had gone to seek that fortune at the court of some native prince, which he could no longer hope for in the British settlements.

CHAPTER 10

Three years passed away after the fatal encounter mentioned in the last Chapter, and Doctor Hartley returning from his appointed mission, which was only temporary, received encouragement to settle in Madras in a medical capacity; and upon having done so, soon had reason to think he had chosen a line in which he might rise to wealth and reputation. His practice was not confined to his countrymen, but much sought after among the natives, who, whatever may be their prejudices against the Europeans in other respects, universally esteem their superior powers in the medical profession. This lucrative branch of practice rendered it necessary that Hartley should make the Oriental languages his study, in order to hold communication with his patients without the intervention of an interpreter. He had enough of opportunities to practise as a linguist, for, in acknowledgment, as he used jocularly to say, of the large fees of the wealthy Moslemah and Hindoos, he attended the poor of all nations gratis, whenever he was called upon.

It so chanced, that one evening he was hastily summoned by a message from the Secretary of the Government, to attend a patient of consequence. "Yet he is, after all, only a Fakir," said the message. "You will find him at the tomb of Cara Razi, the Mahomedan saint and doctor, about one coss from the fort. Enquire for him by the name of Barak el Hadgi. Such a patient promises no fees; but we know how little you care about the pagodas; and, besides, the Government is your paymaster on this occasion."

"That is the last matter to be thought on," said Hartley, and instantly repaired in his palanquin to the place pointed out to him.

The tomb of the Owliah, or Mahomedan Saint, Cara Razi, was a place held in much reverence by every good Mussulman. It was situated in the centre of a grove of mangos and tamarind-trees, and was built of red stone, having three domes, and minarets at every corner. There was a court in front, as usual, around which were cells constructed for the accommodation of the Fakirs who visited the tomb from motives of devotion, and made a longer or shorter residence there as they thought proper, subsisting upon the alms which the Faithful never fail to bestow on them in exchange for the benefit of their prayers. These devotees were engaged day and night in reading verses of the Koran before the tomb, which was constructed of white marble, inscribed with sentences from the book of the Prophet, and with the various titles conferred by the Koran upon the Supreme Being. Such a sepulchre, of which there are many, is, with its appendages and attendants, respected during wars and revolutions, and no less by Feringis, (Franks, that is,) and Hindoos, than by Mahomedans themselves. The Fakirs, in return, act as spies for all parties, and are often employed in secret missions of importance.

Complying with the Mahomedan custom, our friend Hartley laid aside his shoes at the gates of the holy precincts, and avoiding to give offence by approaching near to the tomb, he went up to the principal Moullah, or priest who was distinguishable by the length of his beard, and the size of the large wooden beads, with which the Mahomedans, like the Catholics, keep register of their prayers. Such a person, venerable by his age, sanctity of character, and his real or supposed contempt of worldly pursuits and enjoyments, is regarded as the head of an establishment of this kind.

The Moullah is permitted by his situation to be more communicative with strangers than his younger brethren, who in the present instance remained with their eyes fixed on the Koran, muttering their recitations without noticing the European, or attending to what he said, as he enquired at their superior for Barak el Hadgi.

The Moullah was seated on the earth, from which he did not arise, or show any mark of reverence; nor did he interrupt the tale of his beads, which he continued to count assiduously while Hartley was speaking. When he finished, the old man raised his eyes, and looked at him with an air of distraction, as if he was endeavouring to recollect what he had been saying; he at length pointed to one of the cells, and resumed his devotions like one who felt impatient of whatever withdrew his attention from his sacred duties, were it but for an instant.

Hartley entered the cell indicated, with the usual salutation of Salam Alaikum. His patient lay on a little carpet in a corner of the small white-washed cell. He was a man of about forty, dressed in the black robe of his order, very much torn and patched. He wore a high conical cap of Tartarian felt, and had round his neck the string of black beads belonging to his order. His eyes and posture indicated suffering, which he was enduring with stoical patience.

"Salam Alaikum," said Hartley; "you are in pain, my father?"—a title which he gave rather to the profession than to the years of the person he addressed.

"*Salam Alaikum bema sebastem,*" answered the Fakir; "Well is it for you that you have suffered patiently. The book saith, such shall be the greeting of the angels to those who enter paradise."

The conversation being thus opened, the physician proceeded to enquire into the complaints of the patient, and to prescribe what he thought advisable. Having done this, he was about to retire, when, to his great surprise, the Fakir tendered him a ring of some value.

"The wise," said Hartley, declining the present, and at the same time paying a suitable compliment to the Fakir's cap and robe,—"the wise of every country are brethren. My left hand takes no guerdon of my right."

"A Feringi can then refuse gold?" said the Fakir. "I thought they took it from every hand, whether pure as that of an Houri, or leprous like Gehazi's—even as the hungry dog recketh not whether the flesh he eateth be of the camel of the prophet Saleth, or of the ass of Degial—on whose head be curses!"

"The book says," replied Hartley, "that it is Allah who closes and who enlarges the heart. Frank and Mussulman are all alike moulded by his pleasure."

"My brother hath spoken wisely," answered the patient. "Welcome the disease, if it bring thee acquainted with a wise physician. For what saith the poet—'It is well to have fallen to the earth, if while grovelling there thou shalt discover a diamond.'"

The physician made repeated visits to his patient, and continued to do so even after the health of El Hadgi was entirely restored. He had no difficulty in discerning in him one of those secret agents frequently employed by Asiatic Sovereigns. His intelligence, his learning, above all, his versatility and freedom from prejudices of every kind, left no doubt of Barak's possessing the necessary qualifications for conducting such delicate negotiations; while his gravity of habit and profession could not prevent his features from expressing occasionally a perception of humour, not usually seen in devotees of his class.

Barak el Hadgi talked often, amidst their private conversations, of the power and dignity of the Nawaub of Mysore; and Hartley had little doubt that he came from the Court of Hyder Ali, on some secret mission, perhaps for achieving a more solid peace betwixt that able and sagacious Prince and the East India Company's Government,—that which existed for the time being regarded on both parts as little more than a hollow and insincere truce. He told many stories to the advantage of this Prince, who certainly was one of the wisest that Hindostan could boast; and amidst great crimes, perpetrated to gratify his ambition, displayed many instances of princely generosity, and, what was a little more surprising, of even-handed justice.

On one occasion, shortly before Barak el Hadgi left Madras, he visited the Doctor, and partook of his sherbet, which he preferred to his own, perhaps because a few glasses of rum or brandy were usually added to enrich the compound. It might be owing to repeated applications to the jar which contained this generous fluid, that the Pilgrim became more than usually frank in his communications, and not contented with praising his Nawaub with the most hyperbolic eloquence, he began to insinuate the influence which he himself enjoyed with the Invincible, the Lord and Shield of the Faith of the Prophet.

"Brother of my soul," he said, "do but think if thou needest aught that the all-powerful Hyder Ali Khan Bohander can give; and then use not the intercession of those who dwell in palaces, and wear jewels in their turbans, but seek the cell of thy brother at the Great City, which is Seringapatam. And the poor Fakir, in his torn cloak, shall better advance thy suit with the Nawaub [for Hyder did not assume the title of Sultann] than they who sit upon seats of honour in the Divan."

With these and sundry other expressions of regard, he exhorted Hartley to come into the Mysore, and look upon the face of the Great Prince, whose glance inspired wisdom, and whose nod conferred wealth, so that Folly or Poverty could not appear before him. He offered at the same time to requite the kindness which Hartley had evinced to him, by showing him whatever was worthy the attention of a sage in the land of Mysore.

Hartley was not reluctant to promise to undertake the proposed journey, if the continuance of good understanding betwixt their governments should render it practicable, and in reality looked forward to the possibility of such an event with a good deal of interest. The friends parted with mutual good wishes, after exchanging in the Oriental fashion, such gifts as became sages, to whom knowledge was to be supposed dearer than wealth. Barak el Hadgi presented Hartley with a small quantity of the balsam of Mecca, very hard to be procured in an unadulterated form, and gave him at the same time a passport in a peculiar character, which he assured him would be respected by every officer of the Nawaub, should his friend be disposed to accomplish his visit to the Mysore. "The head of him who should disrespect this safe-conduct," he said, "shall not be more safe than that of the barley-stalk which the reaper has grasped in his hand."

Hartley requited these civilities by the present of a few medicines little used in the East, but such as he thought might, with suitable directions, be safely intrusted to a man so intelligent as his Moslem friend.

It was several months after Barak had returned to the interior of India, that Hartley was astonished by an unexpected rencounter.

The ships from Europe had but lately arrived, and had brought over their usual cargo of boys longing to be commanders, and young women without any purpose of being married, but whom a pious duty to some brother, some uncle, or other male relative, brought to India to keep his house, until they should find themselves unexpectedly in one of their own. Dr. Hartley happened to attend a public breakfast given on this occasion by a gentleman high in the service. The roof of his friend had been recently enriched by a consignment of three nieces, whom the old gentleman, justly attached to his quiet hookah, and, it was said, to a pretty girl of colour, desired to offer to the public, that he might have the fairest chance to get rid of his new guests as soon as possible. Hartley, who was thought a fish worth casting a fly for, was contemplating this fair investment, with very little interest, when he heard one of the company say to another in a low voice,—

"Angels and ministers! there is our old acquaintance, the Queen of Sheba, returned upon our hands like unsaleable goods."

Hartley looked in the same direction with the two who were speaking, and his eye was caught by a Semiramis-looking person, of unusual stature and amplitude, arrayed in a sort of riding-habit, but so formed, and so looped and gallooned with lace, as made it resemble the upper tunic of a native chief. Her robe was composed of crimson silk, rich with flowers of gold. She wore wide trowsers of light blue silk, a fine scarlet shawl around her waist, in which was stuck a creeze with a richly ornamented handle. Her throat and arms were loaded with chains and bracelets, and her turban, formed of a shawl similar to that worn around her waist, was decorated by a magnificent aigrette, from which a blue ostrich plume flowed in one direction, and a red one in another. The brow, of European complexion, on which this tiara rested, was too lofty for beauty, but seemed made for command; the aquiline nose retained its form, but the cheeks were a little sunken, and the complexion so very brilliant, as to give strong evidence that the whole countenance had undergone a thorough repair since the lady had left her couch. A black female slave, richly dressed, stood behind her with a chowry, or cow's tail, having a silver handle, which she used to keep off the flies. From the mode in which she was addressed by those who spoke to her, this lady appeared a person of too much importance to be affronted or neglected, and yet one with whom none desired further communication than the occasion seemed in propriety to demand.

She did not, however, stand in need of attention. The well-known captain of an East Indian vessel lately arrived from Britain was sedulously polite to her; and two or three gentlemen, whom Hartley knew to be engaged in trade, tended upon her as they would have done upon the safety of a rich argosy.

"For Heaven's sake, what is that for a Zenobia?" said Hartley, to the gentleman whose whisper had first attracted his attention to this lofty dame.

"Is it possible you do not know the Queen of Sheba?" said the person of whom he enquired, no way both to communicate the information demanded. "You must know, then, that she is the daughter of a Scotch emigrant, who lived and died at Pondicherry, a sergeant in Lally's regiment. She managed to marry a partisan officer named Montreville, a Swiss or Frenchman, I cannot tell which. After the surrender of Pondicherry, this hero and heroine—But hey—what the devil are you thinking of?—If you stare at her that way, you will make a scene; for she will think nothing of scolding you across the table."

But without attending to his friend's remonstrances, Hartley bolted from the table at which he sat, and made his way, with something less than the decorum which the rules of society enjoin, towards the place where the lady in question was seated.

"The Doctor is surely mad this morning"—said his friend Major Mercer to old Quartermaster Calder.

Indeed, Hartley was not perhaps strictly in his senses; for looking at the Queen of Sheba as he listened to Major Mercer, his eye fell on a light female form beside her, so placed as if she desired to be eclipsed by the bulky form and flowing robes we have described, and to his extreme astonishment, he recognised the friend of his childhood, the love of his youth—Menie Gray herself!

To see her in India was in itself astonishing. To see her apparently under such strange patronage, greatly increased his surprise. To make his way to her, and address her, seemed the natural and direct mode of satisfying the feelings which her appearance excited.

His impetuosity was, however, checked, when, advancing close upon Miss Gray and her companion, he observed that the former, though she looked at him, exhibited not the slightest token of recognition, unless he could interpret as such, that she slightly touched her upper lip with her fore-finger, which, if it happened otherwise than by mere accident, might be construed to mean, "Do not speak to me just now." Hartley, adopting such an interpretation, stood stock still, blushing deeply; for he was aware that he made for the moment but a silly figure.

He was the rather convinced of this, when, with a voice which in the force of its accents corresponded with her commanding air, Mrs. Montreville addressed him in English, which savoured slightly of a Swiss patois,—"You have come to us very fast, sir, to say nothing at all. Are you sure you did not get your tongue stolen by de way?"

"I thought I had seen an old friend in that lady, madam," stammered Hartley, "but it seems I am mistaken."

"The good people do tell me that you are one Doctors Hartley, sir. Now, my friend and I do not know Doctors Hartley at all."

"I have not the presumption to pretend to your acquaintance, madam, but him"—

Here Menie repeated the sign in such a manner, that though it was only momentary, Hartley could not misunderstand its purpose; he therefore changed the end of his sentence, and added, "But I have only to make my bow, and ask pardon for my mistake."

He retired back accordingly among the company, unable to quit the room, and enquiring at those whom he considered as the best newsmongers for such information as—"Who is that stately-looking woman, Mr. Butler?"

"Oh, the Queen of Sheba, to be sure."

"And who is that pretty girl, who sits beside her?"

"Or rather behind her," answered Butler, a military chaplain; "faith, I cannot say—Pretty did you call her?" turning his opera-glass that way—"Yes, faith, she is pretty—very pretty—Gad, she shoots her glances as smartly from behind the old pile yonder, as Teucer from behind Ajax Telamon's shield."

"But who is she, can you tell me?"

"Some fair-skinned speculation of old Montreville's, I suppose, that she has got either to toady herself, or take in some of her black friends with.—Is it possible you have never heard of old Mother Montreville?"

"You know I have been so long absent from Madras"—

"Well," continued Butler, "this lady is the widow of a Swiss officer in the French service, who after the surrender of Pondicherry, went off into the interior, and commenced soldier on his own account. He got possession of a fort, under pretence of keeping it for some simple Rajah or other; assembled around him a parcel of desperate vagabonds, of every colour in the rainbow; occupied a considerable territory, of which he raised the duties in his own name, and declared for independence. But Hyder Naig understood no such interloping proceedings, and down he came, besieged the fort and took it, though some pretend it was betrayed to him by this very woman. Be that as it may, the poor Swiss was found dead on the ramparts. Certain it is, she received large sums of money, under pretence of paying off her troops, surrendering of hill-forts, and Heaven knows what besides. She was permitted also to retain some insignia of royalty; and, as she was wont to talk of Hyder as the Eastern Solomon, she generally became known by the title of Queen of Sheba. She leaves her court when she pleases, and has been as far as Fort St. George before now. In a word, she does pretty much as she likes. The great folks here are civil to her, though they look on her as little better than a spy. As to Hyder, it is supposed he has ensured her fidelity by borrowing the greater part of her treasures, which prevents her from daring to break with him—besides other causes that smack of scandal of another sort."

"A singular story," replied Hartley to his companion, while his heart dwelt on the question, How it was possible that the gentle and simple Menie Gray should be in the train of such a character as this adventuress?

"But Butler has not told you the best of it," said Major Mercer, who by this time came round to finish his own story. "Your old acquaintance, Mr. Tresham, or Mr. Middlemas, or whatever else he chooses to be called, has been complimented by a report, that he stood very high in the good graces of this same Boadicea. He certainly commanded some troops which she stills keeps on foot, and acted at their head in the Nawaub's service, who craftily employed him in whatever could render him odious to his countrymen. The British prisoners were intrusted to his charge, and, to judge by what I felt myself, the devil might take a lesson from him in severity."

"And was he attached to, or connected with, this woman?"

"So Mrs. Rumour told us in our dungeon. Poor Jack Ward had the bastinado for celebrating their merits in a parody on the playhouse song,

'Sure such a pair were never seen,
    So aptly formed to meet by nature.'"

Hartley could listen no longer. The fate of Menie Gray, connected with such a man and such a woman, rushed on his fancy in the most horrid colours, and he was struggling through the throng to get to some place where he might collect his ideas, and consider what could be done for her protection, when a black attendant touched his arm, and at the same time slipped a card into his hand. It bore, "Miss Gray, Mrs. Montreville's, at the house of Ram Sing Cottah, in the Black Town." On the reverse was written with a pencil, "Eight in the morning."

This intimation of her residence implied, of course, a permission, nay, an invitation, to wait upon her at the hour specified. Hartley's heart beat at the idea of seeing her once more, and still more highly at the thought of being able to serve her. At least, he thought, if there is danger near her, as is much to be suspected, she shall not want a counsellor, or, if necessary, a protector. Yet, at the same time, he felt the necessity of making himself better acquainted with the circumstances of her case, and the persons with whom she seemed connected. Butler and Mercer had both spoke to their disparagement; but Butler was a little of a coxcomb, and Mercer a great deal of a gossip. While he was considering what credit was due to their testimony, he was unexpectedly encountered by a gentleman of his own profession, a military surgeon, who had had the misfortune to have been in Hyder's prison, till set at freedom by the late pacification. Mr. Esdale, for so he was called, was generally esteemed a rising man, calm, steady, and deliberate in forming his opinions. Hartley found it easy to turn the subject on the Queen of Sheba, by asking whether her Majesty was not somewhat of an adventuress.

"On my word, I cannot say," answered Esdale, smiling; "we are all upon the adventure in India, more or less; but I do not see that the Begum Montreville is more so than the rest."

"Why, that Amazonian dress and manner," said Hartley, "savour a little of the *picaresca*."

"You must not," said Esdale, "expect a woman who has commanded soldiers, and may again, to dress and look entirely like an ordinary person. But

I assure you, that even at this time of day, if she wished to marry, she might easily find a respectable match."

"Why, I heard that she had betrayed her husband's fort to Hyder."

"Ay, that is a specimen of Madras gossip. The fact is, that she defended the place long after her husband fell, and afterwards surrendered it by capitulation. Hyder, who piques himself on observing the rules of justice, would not otherwise have admitted her to such intimacy."

"Yes, I have heard," replied Hartley, "that their intimacy was rather of the closest."

"Another calumny, if you mean any scandal," answered Esdale. "Hyder is too zealous a Mahomedan to entertain a Christian mistress; and, besides, to enjoy the sort of rank which is yielded to a woman in her condition, she must refrain, in appearance at least, from all correspondence in the way of gallantry. Just so they said that the poor woman had a connexion with poor Middlemas of the—regiment."

"And was that also a false report?" said Hartley, in breathless anxiety.

"On my soul, I believe it was," answered Mr. Esdale. "They were friends, Europeans in an Indian court, and therefore intimate; but I believe nothing more. By the by, though, I believe there was some quarrel between Middlemas, poor fellow, and you; yet I am sure that you will be glad to hear there is a chance of his affair being made up."

"Indeed!" was again the only word which Hartley could utter.

"Ay, indeed," answered Esdale. "The duel is an old story now; and it must be allowed that poor Middlemas, though he was rash in that business, had provocation."

"But his desertion—his accepting of command under Hyder—his treatment of our prisoners—How can all these be passed over?" replied Hartley.

"Why, it is possible—I speak to you as a cautious man, and in confidence—that he may do us better service in Hyder's capital, or Tippoo's camp, than he could have done if serving with his own regiment. And then, for his treatment of prisoners, I am sure I can speak nothing but good of him in that particular. He was obliged to take the office, because those that serve Hyder Naig must do or die. But he told me himself—and I believe him—that he accepted the office chiefly because, while he made a great bullying at us before the black fellows, he could privately be of assistance to us. Some fools could not understand this, and answered him with abuse and lampoons; and he was obliged to punish them, to avoid suspicion. Yes, yes, I and others can prove he was willing to be kind, if men would give him leave. I hope to thank him at Madras one day soon—All this in confidence—Good-morrow to you."

Distracted by the contradictory intelligence he had received, Hartley went next to question old Captain Capstern, the Captain of the Indiaman, whom he had observed in attendance upon the Begum Montreville. On enquiring after that commander's female passengers, he heard a pretty long catalogue of names, in which that he was so much interested in did not occur. On closer enquiry, Capstern recollected that Menie Gray, a young Scotchwoman, had come out under charge of Mrs. Duffer, the master's wife. "A good decent girl," Capstern said, "and kept the mates and guinea-pigs at a respectable distance. She came out," he believed, "to be a sort of female companion, or upper servant in Madame Montreville's family. Snug berth enough," he concluded, "if she can find the length of the old girl's foot."

This was all that could be made of Capstern; so Hartley was compelled to remain in a state of uncertainty until the next morning, when an explanation might be expected with Menie Gray in person.

CHAPTER 11

The exact hour assigned found Hartley at the door of the rich native mer-
chant, who, having some reasons for wishing to oblige the Begum Mon
treville, had relinquished, for her accommodation and that of her numerous
retinue, almost the whole of his large and sumptuous residence in the Black
Town of Madras, as that district of the city is called which the natives occupy.

A domestic, at the first summons, ushered the visitor into an apartment,
where he expected to be joined by Miss Gray. The room opened on one side
into a small garden or parterre, filled with the brilliant-coloured flowers of
Eastern climates; in the midst of which the waters of a fountain rose upwards
in a sparkling jet, and fell back again into a white marble cistern.

A thousand dizzy recollections thronged on the mind of Hartley, whose
early feelings towards the companion of his youth, if they had slumbered during distance and the various casualties of a busy life, were revived when he
found himself placed so near her, and in circumstances which interested from
their unexpected occurrence and mysterious character. A step was heard—
the door opened—a female appeared—but it was the portly form of Madame
de Montreville.

"What do you please to want, sir?" said the lady; "that is, if you have found
your tongue this morning, which you had lost yesterday."

"I proposed myself the honour of waiting upon the young person, whom
I saw in your excellency's company yesterday morning," answered Hartley,
with assumed respect. "I have had long the honour of being known to her in
Europe, and I desire to offer my services to her in India."

"Much obliged—much obliged; but Miss Gray is gone out, and does not
return for one or two days. You may leave your commands with me."

"Pardon me, madam," replied Hartley; "but I have some reason to hope
you may be mistaken in this matter—And here comes the lady herself."

"How is this, my dear?" said Mrs. Montreville, with unruffled front, to Menie, as she entered; "are you not gone out for two or three days, as I tell this gentleman?—*mais c'est egal*—it is all one thing. You will say, How d'ye do, and good-bye, to Monsieur, who is so polite as to come to ask after our healths, and as he sees us both very well, he will go away home again."

"I believe, madam," said Miss Gray, with appearance of effort, "that I must speak with this gentleman for a few minutes in private, if you will permit me."

"That is to say, get you gone? but I do not allow that—I do not like private conversation between young man and pretty young woman; *cela n'est pas honnete*. It cannot be in my house."

"It may be out of it, then, madam," answered Miss Gray, not pettishly nor pertly, but with the utmost simplicity.—"Mr. Hartley, will you step into that garden?—and, you, madam, may observe us from the window, if it be the fashion of the country to watch so closely."

As she spoke this she stepped through a lattice-door into the garden, and with an air so simple, that she seemed as if she wished to comply with her patroness's ideas of decorum, though they appeared strange to her. The Queen of Sheba, notwithstanding her natural assurance, was disconcerted by the composure of Miss Gray's manner, and left the room, apparently in displeasure. Menie turned back to the door which opened into the garden, and said in the same manner as before, but with less nonchalance,—

"I am sure I would not willingly break through the rules of a foreign country; but I cannot refuse myself the pleasure of speaking to so old a friend,—if indeed," she added, pausing and looking at Hartley, who was much embarrassed, "it be as much pleasure to Mr. Hartley as it is to me."

"It would have been," said Hartley, scarce knowing what he said—"it must be a pleasure to me in every circumstance—But this extraordinary meeting—But your father"—

Menie Gray's handkerchief was at her eyes.—"He is gone, Mr. Hartley. After he was left unassisted, his toilsome business became too much for him—he caught a cold which hung about him, as you know he was the last to attend to his own complaints, till it assumed a dangerous, and, finally, a fatal character. I distress you, Mr. Hartley, but it becomes you well to be affected. My father loved you dearly."

"Oh, Miss Gray!" said Hartley, "it should not have been thus with my excellent friend at the close of his useful and virtuous life—Alas, wherefore— the question bursts from me involuntarily—wherefore could you not have complied with his wishes?—wherefore"—

"Do not ask me," said she, stopping the question which was on his lips; "we are not the formers of our own destiny. It is painful to talk on such a subject; but for once, and for ever, let me tell you that I should have done Mr.

Hartley wrong, if, even to secure his assistance to my father, I had accepted his hand, while my wayward affections did not accompany the act."

"But wherefore do I see you here, Menie?—Forgive me, Miss Gray, my tongue as well as my heart turns back to long-forgotten scenes—But why here?—why with this woman?"

"She is not, indeed, every thing that I expected," answered Menie; "but I must not be prejudiced by foreign manners, after the step I have taken—She is, besides, attentive, and generous in her way, and I shall soon"—she paused a moment, and then added, "be under better protection."

"That of Richard Middlemas?" said Hartley with a faltering voice.

"I ought not, perhaps, to answer the question," said Menie; "but I am a bad dissembler, and those whom I trust, I trust entirely. You have guessed right, Mr. Hartley," she added,—colouring a good deal, "I have come hither to unite my fate to that of your old comrade."

"It is, then, just as I feared!" exclaimed Hartley.

"And why should Mr. Hartley fear?" said Menie Gray. "I used to think you too generous—surely the quarrel which occurred long since ought not to perpetuate suspicion and resentment."

"At least, if the feeling of resentment remained in my own bosom, it would be the last I should intrude upon you, Miss Gray," answered Hartley. "But it is for you, and for you alone, that I am watchful.—This person—this gentleman whom you mean to intrust with your happiness—do you know where he is—and in what service?"

"I know both, more distinctly perhaps than Mr. Hartley can do. Mr. Middlemas has erred greatly, and has been severely punished. But it was not in the time of his exile and sorrow, that she who has plighted her faith to him should, with the flattering world, turn her back upon him. Besides, you have, doubtless, not heard of his hopes of being restored to his country and his rank?"

"I have," answered Hartley, thrown off his guard; "but I see not how he can deserve it, otherwise than by becoming a traitor to his new master, and thus rendering himself even more unworthy of confidence than I hold him to be at this moment."

"It is well that he hears you not," answered Menie Gray, resenting, with natural feeling, the imputation on her lover. Then instantly softening her tone she added, "My voice ought not to aggravate, but to soothe your quarrel. Mr. Hartley, I plight my word to you that you do Richard wrong."

She said these words with affected calmness, suppressing all appearance of that displeasure, of which she was evidently sensible, upon this deprecia-tion of a beloved object.

Hartley compelled himself to answer in the same strain.

"Miss Gray," he said, "your actions and motives will always be those of an angel; but let me entreat you to view this most important matter with the eyes of worldly wisdom and prudence. Have you well weighed the risks attending the course which you are taking in favour of a man, who,—nay, I will not again offend you—who may, I hope, deserve your favour?"

"When I wished to see you in this manner, Mr. Hartley, and declined a communication in public, where we could have had less freedom of conversation, it was with the view of telling you every thing. Some pain I thought old recollections might give, but I trusted it would be momentary; and, as I desire to retain your friendship, it is proper I should show that I still deserve it. I must then first tell you my situation after my father's death. In the world's opinion we were always poor, you know; but in the proper sense I had not known what real poverty was, until I was placed in dependence upon a distant relation of my poor father, who made our relationship a reason for casting upon me all the drudgery of her household, while she would not allow that it gave me a claim to countenance, kindness, or anything but the relief of my most pressing wants. In these circumstances I received from Mr. Middlemas a letter, in which he related his fatal duel, and its consequences. He had not dared to write to me to share his misery—Now, when he was in a lucrative situation, under the patronage of a powerful prince, whose wisdom knew how to prize and protect such Europeans as entered his service—now, when he had every prospect of rendering our government such essential service by his interest with Hyder Ali, and might eventually nourish hopes of being permitted to return and stand his trial for the death of his commanding officer—now, he pressed me to come to India, and share his reviving fortunes, by accomplishing the engagement into which we had long ago entered. A considerable sum of money accompanied this letter. Mrs. Duffer was, pointed out as a respectable woman, who would protect me during the passage. Mrs. Montreville, a lady of rank, having large possessions and high interest in the Mysore, would receive me on my arrival at Fort St. George, and conduct me safely to the dominions of Hyder. It was farther recommended, that, considering the peculiar situation of Mr. Middlemas, his name should be concealed in the transaction, and that the ostensible cause of my voyage should be to fill an office in that lady's family—What was I to do?—My duty to my poor father was ended, and my other friends considered the proposal as too advantageous to be rejected. The references given, the sum of money lodged, were considered as putting all scruples out of the question, and my immediate protectress and kinswoman was so earnest that I should accept of the offer made me, as to intimate that she would not encourage me to stand in my own light, by continuing to give me shelter and food, (she gave me little more,) if I was foolish enough to refuse compliance."

"Sordid wretch!" said Hartley, "how little did she deserve such a charge!"

"Let me speak a proud word, Mr. Hartley, and then you will not perhaps blame my relations so much. All their persuasions, and even their threats, would have failed in inducing me to take a step, which has an appearance, at least, to which I found it difficult to reconcile myself. But I had loved Middlemas—I love him still—why should I deny it?—and I have not hesitated to trust him. Had it not been for the small still voice which reminded me of my engagements, I had maintained more stubbornly the pride of womanhood, and, as you would perhaps have recommended, I might have expected, at least, that my lover should have come to Britain in person, and might have had the vanity to think," she added, smiling faintly, "that if I were worth having, I was worth fetching."

"Yet now—even now," answered Hartley, "be just to yourself while you are generous to your lover.—Nay, do not look angrily, but hear me. I doubt the propriety of your being under the charge of this unsexed woman, who can no longer be termed a European. I have interest enough with females of the highest rank in the settlement—this climate is that of generosity and hospitality—there is not one of them, who, knowing your character and history, will not desire to have you in her society, and under her protection, until your lover shall be able to vindicate his title to your hand in the face of the world.—I myself will be no cause of suspicion to him, or of inconvenience to you, Menie. Let me but have your consent to the arrangement I propose, and the same moment that sees you under honourable and unsuspected protection, I will leave Madras, not to return till your destiny is in one way or other permanently fixed."

"No, Hartley," said Miss Gray. "It may, it must be, friendly in you thus to advise me; but it would be most base in me to advance my own affairs at the expense of your prospects. Besides, what would this be but taking the chance of contingencies, with the view of sharing poor Middlemas's fortunes, should they prove prosperous, and casting him off, should they be otherwise? Tell me only, do you, of your own positive knowledge, aver that you consider this woman as an unworthy and unfit protectress for so young a person as I am?"

"Of my own knowledge I can say nothing; nay, I must own, that reports differ even concerning Mrs. Montreville's character. But surely the mere suspicion"—

"The mere suspicion, Mr. Hartley, can have no weight with me, considering that I can oppose to it the testimony of the man with whom I am willing to share my future fortunes. You acknowledge the question is but doubtful, and should not the assertion of him of whom I think so highly decide my belief in a doubtful matter? What, indeed, must he be, should this Madame Montreville be other than he represented her?"

"What must he be, indeed!" thought Hartley internally, but his lips uttered not the words. He looked down in a deep reverie, and at length started from it at the words of Miss Gray.

"It is time to remind you, Mr. Hartley, that we must needs part. God bless and preserve you."

"And you, dearest Menie," exclaimed Hartley as he sunk on one knee, and pressed to his lips the hand which she held out to him. "God bless you!—you must deserve blessing. God protect you!—you must need protection.—Oh, should things prove different from what you hope, send for me instantly, and if man can aid you, Adam Hartley will!"

He placed in her hand a card containing his address. He then rushed from the apartment. In the hall he met the lady of the mansion, who made him a haughty reverence in token of adieu, while a native servant of the upper class, by whom she was attended, made a low and reverential salam.

Hartley hastened from the Black Town, more satisfied than before that some deceit was about to be practised towards Menie Gray—more determined than ever to exert himself for her preservation; yet more completely perplexed, when he began to consider the doubtful character of the danger to which she might be exposed, and the scanty means of protection which she had to oppose to it.

CHAPTER 12

As Hartley left the apartment in the house of Ram Sing Cottah by one mode of exit, Miss Gray retired by another, to an apartment destined for her private use. She, too, had reason for secret and anxious reflection, since all her love for Middlemas, and her full confidence in his honour, could not entirely conquer her doubts concerning the character of the person whom he had chosen for her temporary protectress. And yet she could not rest these doubts upon any thing distinctly conclusive; it was rather a dislike of her patroness's general manners, and a disgust at her masculine notions and expressions, that displeased her, than any thing else.

Meantime, Madame Montreville, followed by her black domestic, entered the apartment where Hartley and Menie had just parted. It appeared from the conversation which follows, that they had from some place of concealment overheard the dialogue we have narrated in the former chapter.

"It is good luck, Sadoc," said the lady, "that there is in this world the great fool."

"And the great villain," answered Sadoc, in good English, but in a most sullen tone.

"This woman, now," continued the lady, "is what in Frangistan you call an angel."

"Ay, and I have seen those in Hindostan you may well call devil."

"I am sure that this—how you call him—Hartley, is a meddling devil. For what has he to do? She will not have any of him. What is his business who has her? I wish we were well up the Ghauts again, my dear Sadoc."

"For my part," answered the slave, "I am half determined never to ascend the Ghauts more. Hark you, Adela, I begin to sicken of the plan we have laid. This creature's confiding purity—call her angel or woman, as you will—makes my practices appear too vile, even in my own eyes. I feel myself unfit to be your companion farther in the daring paths which you pursue. Let us part, and part friends."

"Amen, coward. But the woman remains with me," answered the Queen of Sheba.[11]

"With thee!" replied the seeming black—"never. No, Adela. She is under the shadow of the British flag, and she shall experience its protection."

"Yes—and what protection will it afford to you yourself?" retorted the Amazon. "What if I should clap my hands, and command a score of my black servants to bind you like a sheep, and then send word to the Governor of the Presidency that one Richard Middlemas, who had been guilty of mutiny, murder, desertion, and serving of the enemy against his countrymen, is here, at Ram Sing Cottah's house, in the disguise of a black servant?" Middlemas covered his face with his hands, while Madame Montreville proceeded to load him with reproaches.—"Yes," she said, "slave and son of a slave! Since you wear the dress of my household, you shall obey me as fully as the rest of them, otherwise,—whips, fetters,—the scaffold, renegade,—the gallows, murderer! Dost thou dare to reflect on the abyss of misery from which I raised thee, to share my wealth and my affections? Dost thou not remember that the picture of this pale, cold, unimpassioned girl was then so indifferent to thee, that thou didst sacrifice it as a tribute due to the benevolence of her who relieved thee, to the affection of her who, wretch as thou art, condescended to love thee?"

"Yes, fell woman," answered Middlemas, "but was it I who encouraged the young tyrant's outrageous passion for a portrait, or who formed the abominable plan of placing the original within his power?"

"No—for to do so required brain and wit. But it was thine, flimsy villain, to execute the device which a bolder genius planned; it was thine to entice the woman to this foreign shore, under pretence of a love, which, on thy part, cold-blooded miscreant, never had existed."

"Peace, screech-owl!" answered Middlemas, "nor drive me to such madness as may lead me to forget thou art a woman."

"A woman, dastard! Is this thy pretext for sparing me?—what, then, art thou, who tremblest at a woman's looks, a woman's words?—I am a woman, renegade, but one who wears a dagger, and despises alike thy strength and thy courage. I am a woman who has looked on more dying men than thou hast killed deer and antelopes. Thou must traffic for greatness?—thou hast thrust thyself like a five-years' child, into the rough sports of men, and wilt only be borne down and crushed for thy pains. Thou wilt be a double traitor, forsooth—betray thy betrothed to the Prince, in order to obtain the means of betraying

---

11 In order to maintain uninjured the tone of passion throughout this dialogue, it has been judged expedient to discard, in the Language of the Begum, the *patois* of Madame Munreville.

the Prince to the English, and thus gain thy pardon from thy countrymen. But me thou shalt not betray. I will not be made the tool of thy ambition—I will not give thee the aid of my treasures and my soldiers, to be sacrificed at last to this northern icicle. No, I will watch thee as the fiend watches the wizard. Show but a symptom of betraying me while we are here, and I denounce thee to the English, who might pardon the successful villain, but not him who can only offer prayers for his life, in place of useful services. Let me see thee flinch when we are beyond the Ghauts, and the Nawaub shall know thy intrigues with the Nizam and the Mahrattas, and thy resolution to deliver up Bangalore to the English, when the imprudence of Tippoo shall have made thee Killedar. Go where thou wilt, slave, thou shalt find me thy mistress."

"And a fair though an unkind one," said the counterfeit Sadoc, suddenly changing his tone to an affectation of tenderness. "It is true I pity this unhappy woman; true I would save her if I could—but most unjust to suppose I would in any circumstances prefer her to my Nourjehan, my light of the world, my Mootee Mahul, my pearl of the palace"—

"All false coin and empty compliment," said the Begum. "Let me hear, in two brief words, that you leave this woman to my disposal."

"But not to be interred alive under your seat, like the Circassian of whom you were jealous," said Middlemas, shuddering.

"No, fool; her lot shall not be worse than that of being the favourite of a prince. Hast thou, fugitive and criminal as thou art, a better fate to offer her?"

"But," replied Middlemas, blushing even through his base disguise at the consciousness of his abject conduct, "I will have no force on her inclinations."

"Such truce she shall have as the laws of the Zenana allow," replied the female tyrant. "A week is long enough for her to determine whether she will be the willing mistress of a princely and generous lover."

"Ay," said Richard, "and before that week expires"—He stopped short.

"What will happen before the week expires?" said the Begum Montreville.

"No matter—nothing of consequence. I leave the woman's fate with you."

"'Tis well—we march to-night on our return, so soon as the moon rises Give orders to our retinue."

"To hear is to obey," replied the seeming slave, and left the apartment.

The eyes of the Begum remained fixed on the door through which he had passed. "Villain—double-dyed villain!" she said, "I see thy drift; thou wouldst betray Tippoo, in policy alike and in love. But me thou canst betray.—Ho, there, who waits? Let a trusty messenger be ready to set off instantly with letters, which I will presently make ready. His departure must be a secret to every one.—And now shall this pale phantom soon know her destiny, and learn what it is to have rivalled Adela Montreville."

While the Amazonian Princess meditated plans of vengeance against her innocent rival and the guilty lover, the latter plotted as deeply for his own purposes. He had waited until such brief twilight as India enjoys rendered his disguise complete, then set out in haste for the part of Madras inhabited by the Europeans, or, as it is termed, Fort St. George.

"I will save her yet," he said; "ere Tippoo can seize his prize, we will raise around his ears a storm which would drive the God of War from the arms of the Goddess of Beauty. The trap shall close its fangs upon this Indian tiger, ere he has time to devour the bait which enticed him into the snare."

While Middlemas cherished these hopes, he approached the Residency. The sentinel on duty stopped him, as of course, but he was in possession of the counter-sign, and entered without opposition. He rounded the building in which the President of the Council resided, an able and active, but unconscientious man, who, neither in his own affairs, nor in those of the Company, was supposed to embarrass himself much about the means which he used to attain his object. A tap at a small postern gate was answered by a black slave, who admitted Middlemas to that necessary appurtenance of every government, a back stair, which, in its turn, conducted him to the office of the Bramin Paupiah, the Dubash, or steward of the great man, and by whose means chiefly he communicated with the native courts, and carried on many mysterious intrigues, which he did not communicate to his brethren at the council-board.

It is perhaps justice to the guilty and unhappy Middlemas to suppose, that if the agency of a British officer had been employed, he might have been induced to throw himself on his mercy, might have explained the whole of his nefarious bargain with Tippoo, and, renouncing his guilty projects of ambition, might have turned his whole thoughts upon saving Menie Gray, ere she was transported beyond the reach of British protection. But the thin dusky form which stood before him, wrapped in robes of muslin embroidered with gold, was that of Paupiah, known as a master-counsellor of dark projects, an Oriental Machiavel, whose premature wrinkles were the result of many an intrigue, in which the existence of the poor, the happiness of the rich, the honour of men, and the chastity of women, had been sacrificed without scruple, to attain some private or political advantage. He did not even enquire by what means the renegade Briton proposed to acquire that influence with Tippoo which might enable him to betray him—he only desired to be assured that the fact was real.

"You speak at the risk of your head, if you deceive Paupiah, or make Paupiah the means of deceiving his master. I know, so does all Madras, that the Nawaub has placed his young son, Tippoo, as Vice-Regent of his newly-conquered territory of Bangalore, which Hyder hath lately added to his dominions. But that Tippoo should bestow the government of that important place on an apostate Feringi, seems more doubtful."

"Tippoo is young," answered Middlemas, "and to youth the temptation of the passions is what a lily on the surface of the lake is to childhood—they will risk life to reach it, though, when obtained, it is of little value. Tippoo has the cunning of his father and his military talents, but he lacks his cautious wisdom."

"Thou speakest truth—but when thou art Governor of Bangalore, hast thou forces to hold the place till thou art relieved by the Mahrattas, or by the British?"

"Doubt it not—the soldiers of the Begum Mootee Mahul, whom the Europeans call Montreville, are less hers than mine. I am myself her Bukshee, [General,] and her Sirdars are at my devotion. With these I could keep Bangalore for two months, and the British army may be before it in a week. What do you risk by advancing General Smith's army nearer to the frontier?"

"We risk a settled peace with Hyder," answered Paupiah, "for which he has made advantageous offers. Yet I say not but thy plan may be most advantageous. Thou sayest Tippoo's treasures are in the fort?"

"His treasures and his Zenana; I may even be able to secure his person."

"That were a goodly pledge," answered the Hindoo minister.

"And you consent that the treasures shall be divided to the last rupee, as in the scroll?"

"The share of Paupiah's master is too small," said the Bramin; "and the name of Paupiah is unnoticed."

"The share of the Begum may be divided between Paupiah and his master," answered Middlemas.

"But the Begum will expect her proportion," replied Paupiah.

"Let me alone to deal with her," said Middlemas. "Before the blow is struck, she shall not know of our private treaty, and afterwards her disappointment will be of little consequence. And now, remember my stipulations—my rank to be restored—my full pardon to be granted."

"Ay," replied Paupiah, cautiously, "should you succeed. But were you to betray what has here passed, I will find the dagger of a Lootie which shall reach thee, wert thou sheltered under the folds of the Nawaub's garment. In the meantime, take this missive, and when you are in possession of Bangalore, despatch it to General Smith, whose division shall have orders to approach as near the frontiers of Mysore as may be, without causing suspicion."

Thus parted this worthy pair; Paupiah to report to his principal the progress of these dark machinations, Middlemas to join the Begum, on her return to the Mysore. The gold and diamonds of Tippoo, the importance which he was about to acquire, the ridding himself at once of the capricious authority of the irritable Tippoo, and the troublesome claims of the Begum, were such agreeable subjects of contemplation, that he scarcely thought of the fate of his European victim,—unless to salve his conscience with the hope that the sole injury she could sustain might be the alarm of a few days, during the course of which he would acquire the means of delivering her from the tyrant, in whose

Zenana she was to remain a temporary prisoner. He resolved, at the same time, to abstain from seeing her till the moment he could afford her protection, justly considering the danger which his whole plan might incur, if he again awakened the jealousy of the Begum. This he trusted was now asleep; and, in the course of their return to Tippoo's camp, near Bangalore, it was his study to soothe this ambitious and crafty female by blandishments, intermingled with the more splendid prospects of wealth and power to be opened to them both, as he pretended, by the success of his present enterprise.[12]

---

12 It is scarce necessary to say, that such things could only be acted in the earlier period of our Indian settlements, when the check of the Directors was imperfect, and that of the crown did not exist. My friend Mr. Fairscribe is of opinion, that there is an anachronism in the introduction of Paupiah, the Bramin Dubash of the English governor.—C. C.

CHAPTER 13

It appears that the jealous and tyrannical Begum did not long suspend her purpose of agonizing her rival by acquainting her with her intended fate. By prayers or rewards, Menie Gray prevailed on a servant of Ram Sing Cottah, to deliver to Hartley the following distracted note:—

> "All is true your fears foretold—He has delivered me up to a cruel woman, who threatens to sell me to the tyrant, Tippoo. Save me if you can—if you have not pity, or cannot give me aid, there is none left upon earth.—
>
> M. G."

The haste with which Dr. Hartley sped to the Fort, and demanded an audience of the Governor, was defeated by the delays interposed by Paupiah.

It did not suit the plans of this artful Hindoo, that any interruption should be opposed to the departure of the Begum and her favourite, considering how much the plans of the last corresponded with his own. He affected incredulity on the charge, when Hartley complained of an Englishwoman being detained in the train of the Begum against her consent, treated the complaint of Miss Gray as the result of some female quarrel unworthy of particular attention, and when at length he took some steps for examining further into the matter, he contrived they should be so tardy, that the Begum and her retinue were far beyond the reach of interruption.

Hartley let his indignation betray him into reproaches against Paupiah, in which his principal was not spared. This only served to give the impassable Bramin a pretext for excluding him from the Residency, with a hint, that if his language continued to be of such an imprudent character, he might expect to be removed from Madras, and stationed at some hillfort or village among the mountains, where his medical knowledge would find full exercise in protecting himself and others from the unhealthiness of the climate.

As he retired, bursting with ineffectual indignation, Esdale was the first person whom Hartley chanced to meet with, and to him, stung with impatience, he communicated what he termed the infamous conduct of the Governor's Dubash, connived at, as he had but too much reason to suppose, by the Governor himself; exclaiming against the want of spirit which they betrayed, in abandoning a British subject to the fraud of renegades, and the force of a tyrant.

Esdale listened with that sort of anxiety which prudent men betray when they feel themselves like to be drawn into trouble by the discourse of an imprudent friend.

"If you desire to be personally righted in this matter," said he at length, "you must apply to Leadenhall Street, where I suspect—betwixt ourselves—complaints are accumulating fast, both against Paupiah and his master."

"I care for neither of them," said Hartley; "I need no personal redress—I desire none—I only want succour for Menie Gray."

"In that case," said Esdale, "you have only one resource—you must apply to Hyder himself"—

"To Hyder—to the usurper—the tyrant?"

"Yes, to this usurper and tyrant," answered Esdale, "you must be contented to apply. His pride is, to be thought a strict administrator of justice; and perhaps he may on this, as on other occasions, choose to display himself in the light of an impartial magistrate."

"Then I go to demand justice at his footstool," said Hartley.

"Not so fast, my dear Hartley," answered his friend; "first consider the risk. Hyder is just by reflection, and perhaps from political considerations; but by temperament, his blood is as unruly as ever beat under a black skin, and if you do not find him in the vein of judging, he is likely enough to be in that of killing. Stakes and bowstrings are as frequently in his head as the adjustment of the scales of justice."

"No matter—I will instantly present myself at his Durbar. The Governor cannot for very shame refuse me letters of credence."

"Never think of asking them," said his more experienced friend; "it would cost Paupiah little to have them so worded as to induce Hyder to rid our sable Dubash, at once and for ever, of the sturdy free-spoken Dr. Adam Hartley. A Vakeel, or messenger of government, sets out to-morrow for Seringapatam; contrive to join him on the road, his passport will protect you both. Do you know none of the chiefs about Hyder's person?"

"None, excepting his late emissary to this place, Barak el Hadgi," answered Hartley.

"His support," said Esdale, "although only a Fakir, may be as effectual as that of persons of more essential consequence. And, to say the truth, where the caprice of a despot is the question in debate, there is no knowing upon what it is best to reckon.—Take my advice, my dear Hartley, leave this poor girl to her fate. After all, by placing yourself in an attitude of endeavouring to save her, it is a hundred to one that you only ensure your own destruction."

Hartley shook his head, and bade Esdale hastily farewell; leaving him in the happy and self-applauding state of mind proper to one who has given the best advice possible to a friend, and may conscientiously wash his hands of all consequences.

Having furnished himself with money, and with the attendance of three trusty native servants, mounted like himself on Arab horses, and carrying with them no tent, and very little baggage, the anxious Hartley lost not a moment in taking the road to Mysore, endeavouring, in the meantime, by recollecting every story he had ever heard of Hyder's justice and forbearance, to assure himself that he should find the Nawaub disposed to protect a helpless female, even against, the future heir of his empire.

Before he crossed the Madras territory, he overtook the Vakeel, or messenger of the British Government, of whom Esdale had spoken. This man, accustomed for a sum of money to permit adventurous European traders who desired to visit Hyder's capital, to share his protection, passport, and escort, was not disposed to refuse the same good office to a gentleman of credit at Madras; and, propitiated by an additional gratuity, undertook to travel as speedily as possible. It was a journey which was not prosecuted without much fatigue and considerable danger, as they had to traverse a country frequently exposed to all the evils of war, more especially when they approached the Ghauts, those tremendous mountain-passes which descend from the tableland of Mysore, and through which the mighty streams that arise in the centre of the Indian peninsula, find their way to the ocean.

The sun had set ere the party reached the foot of one of these perilous passes, up which lay the road to Seringapatam. A narrow path, which in summer resembled an empty water-course, winding upwards among immense rocks and precipices, was at one time completely overshadowed by dark groves of teak-trees, and at another, found its way beside impenetrable jungles, the habitation of jackals and tigers.

By means of this unsocial path the travellers threaded their way in silence,—Hartley, whose impatience kept him before the Vakeel, eagerly enquiring when the moon would enlighten the darkness, which, after the sun's disappearance, closed fast around them. He was answered by the natives according to their usual mode of expression, that the moon was in her dark side, and that he was not to hope to behold her bursting through a cloud to illuminate the thickets and strata of black and slaty rocks, amongst which they were winding. Hartley had therefore no resource, save to keep his eye steadily fixed on the lighted match of the Sowar, or horseman, who rode before him, which, for sufficient reasons, was always kept in readiness to be applied to the priming of the matchlock. The vidette, on his part, kept a watchful eye on the Dowrah, a guide supplied at the last village, who, having got more than halfway from his own house, was much to be suspected of meditating how to escape the trouble of going further.[13]

The Dowrah, on the other hand, conscious of the lighted match and loaded gun behind him, hollowed from time to time to show that he was on his duty, and to accelerate the march of the travellers. His cries were answered by an occasional ejaculation of Ulla from the black soldiers, who closed the rear, and who were meditating on former adventures, the plundering of a *Kaffila*, (party of travelling merchants,) or some such exploit, or perhaps reflecting that a tiger, in the neighboring jungle, might be watching patiently for the last of the party, in order to spring upon him, according to his usual practice.

The sun, which appeared almost as suddenly as it had left them, served to light the travellers in the remainder of the ascent, and called forth from the Mahomedans belonging to the party the morning prayer of Alla Akber, which resounded in long notes among the rocks and ravines, and they continued with better advantage their forced march until the pass opened upon a boundless extent of jungle, with a single high mud fort rising through the midst of it. Upon this plain rapine and war had suspended the labours of industry, and the rich vegetation of the soil had in a few years converted a fertile champaign country into an almost impenetrable thicket. Accordingly, the banks of a small nullah, or brook, were covered with the footmarks of tigers and other animals of prey.

Here the travellers stopped to drink, and to refresh themselves and their horses; and it was near this spot that Hartley saw a sight which forced him to compare the subject which engrossed his own thoughts, with the distress that had afflicted another.

At a spot not far distant from the brook, the guide called their attention to a most wretched looking man, overgrown with hair, who was seated on the skin of a tiger. His body was covered with mud and ashes, his skin sunburnt, his dress a few wretched tatters. He appeared not to observe the approach of the strangers, neither moving nor speaking a word, but remaining with his eyes fixed on a small and rude tomb, formed of the black slate stones which lay around, and exhibiting a small recess for a lamp. As they approached the man, and placed before him a rupee or two, and some rice, they observed that a tiger's skull and bones lay beside him, with a sabre almost consumed by rust.

---

13 In every village the Dowrah, or Guide, is an official person, upon the public establishment, and receives a portion of the harvest or other revenue, along with the Smith, the Sweeper, and the Barber. As he gets nothing from the travellers whom it is his office to conduct, he never scruples to shorten his own journey and prolong theirs by taking them to the nearest village, without reference to the most direct line of route, and sometimes deserts them entirely. If the regular Dowrah is sick or absent, no wealth can procure a substitute.

While they gazed on this miserable object, the guide acquainted them with his tragical history. Sadhu Sing had been a Sipahee, or soldier, and free-booter of course, the native and the pride of a half-ruined village which they had passed on the preceding day. He was betrothed to the daughter of a Si-pahee, who served in the mud fort which they saw at a distance rising above the jungle. In due time, Sadhu, with his friends, came for the purpose of the marriage, and to bring home the bride. She was mounted on a Tatoo, a small horse belonging to the country, and Sadhu and his friends preceded her on foot, in all their joy and pride. As they approached the nullah near which the travellers were resting, there was heard a dreadful roar, accompanied by a shriek of agony. Sadhu Sing, who instantly turned, saw no trace of his bride, save that her horse ran wild in one direction, whilst in the other the long grass and reeds of the jungle were moving like the ripple of the ocean, when dis-torted by the course of a shark holding its way near the surface. Sadhu drew his sabre and rushed forward in that direction; the rest of the party remained motionless until roused by a short roar of agony. They then plunged into the jungle with their drawn weapons, where they speedily found Sadhu Sing holding in his arms the lifeless corpse of his bride, where a little farther lay the body of the tiger, slain by such a blow over the neck as desperation itself could alone have discharged.—The brideless bridegroom would permit none to interfere with his sorrow. He dug a grave for his Mora, and erected over it the rude tomb they saw, and never afterwards left the spot. The beasts of prey themselves seemed to respect or dread the extremity of his sorrow. His friends brought him food and water from the nullah, but he neither smiled nor showed any mark of acknowledgment, unless when they brought him flowers to deck the grave of Mora. Four or five years, according to the guide, had passed away, and there Sadhu Sing still remained among the trophies of his grief and his vengeance, exhibiting all the symptoms of advanced age, though still in the prime of youth. The tale hastened the travellers from their resting-place; the Vakeel because it reminded him of the dangers of the jungle, and Hartley because it coincided too well with the probable fate of his be-loved, almost within the grasp of a more formidable tiger than that whose skeleton lay beside Sadhu Sing.

It was at the mud fort already mentioned that the travellers received the first accounts of the progress of the Begum and her party, by a Peon (or foot-soldier) who had been in their company, but was now on his return to the coast. They had travelled, he said, with great speed, until they ascended the Ghauts, where they were joined by a party of the Begum's own forces; and he and others, who had been brought from Madras as a temporary escort, were paid and dismissed to their homes. After this, he understood it was the pur-pose of the Begum Mootee Mahul, to proceed by slow marches and frequent halts, to Bangalore, the vicinity of which place she did not desire to reach until Prince Tippoo, with whom she desired an interview, should have returned from an expedition towards Vandicotta, in which he had lately been engaged.

From the result of his anxious enquiries, Hartley had reason to hope, that though Seringapatam was seventy-five miles more to the eastward than Bangalore, yet, by using diligence, he might have time to throw himself at the feet of Hyder, and beseech his interposition, before the meeting betwixt Tippoo and the Begum should decide the fate of Menie Gray. On the other hand, he trembled as the Peon told him that the Begum's Bukshee, or General, who had travelled to Madras with her in disguise, had now assumed the dress and character belonging to his rank, and it was expected he was to be honoured by the Mahomedan Prince with some high office of dignity. With still deeper anxiety, he learned that a palanquin, watched with sedulous care by the slaves of Oriental jealousy, contained, it was whispered, a Feringi, or Frankish woman, beautiful as a Houri, who had been brought from England by the Begum, as a present to Tippoo. The deed of villany was therefore in full train to be accomplished; it remained to see whether by diligence on Hartley's side, its course could be interrupted.

When this eager vindicator of betrayed innocence arrived in the capital of Hyder, it may be believed that he consumed no time in viewing the temple of the celebrated Vishnoo, or in surveying the splendid Gardens called Lollbang, which were the monument of Hyder's magnificence, and now hold his mortal remains. On the contrary, he was no sooner arrived in the city, than he hastened to the principal Mosque, having no doubt that he was there most likely to learn some tidings of Barak el Hadgi. He approached accordingly the sacred spot, and as to enter it would have cost a Feringi his life, he employed the agency of a devout Mussulman to obtain information concerning the person whom he sought. He was not long in learning that the Fakir Barak was within the Mosque, as he had anticipated, busied with his holy office of reading passages from the Koran, and its most approved commentators. To interrupt him in his devout task was impossible, and it was only by a high bribe that he could prevail on the same Moslem whom he had before employed, to slip into the sleeve of the holy man's robe a paper containing his name, and that of the Khan in which the Vakeel had taken up his residence. The agent brought back for answer, that the Fakir, immersed, as was to be expected, in the holy service which he was in the act of discharging, had paid no visible attention to the symbol of intimation which the Feringi Sahib [European gentleman] had sent to him. Distracted with the loss of time, of which each moment was precious, Hartley next endeavoured to prevail on the Mussulman to interrupt the Fakir's devotions with a verbal message; but the man was indignant at the very proposal.

"Dog of a Christian!" he said, "what art thou and thy whole generation, that Barak el Hadgi should lose a divine thought for the sake of an infidel like thee?"

Exasperated beyond self-possession, the unfortunate Hartley was now about to intrude upon the precincts of the Mosque in person, in hopes of interrupting the formal prolonged recitation which issued from its recesses, when an old man laid his hand on his shoulder, and prevented him from a rashness which might have cost him his life, saying, at the same time, "You are a Sahib Angrezie, [English gentleman;] I have been a Telinga [a private soldier] in the Company's service, and have eaten their salt. I will do your errand for you to the Fakir Barak el Hadgi."

So saying, he entered the Mosque, and presently returned with the Fakir's answer, in these enigmatical words:—"He who would see the sun rise must watch till the dawn."

With this poor subject of consolation, Hartley retired to his inn, to meditate on the futility of the professions of the natives, and to devise some other mode of finding access to Hyder than that which he had hitherto trusted to. On this point, however, he lost all hope, being informed by his late fellow-traveller, whom he found at the Khan, that the Nawaub was absent from the city on a secret expedition, which might detain him for two or three days. This was the answer which the Vakeel himself had received from the Dewan, with a farther intimation, that he must hold himself ready, when he was required, to deliver his credentials to Prince Tippoo, instead of the Nawaub; his business being referred to the former, in a way not very promising for the success of his mission.

Hartley was now nearly thrown into despair. He applied to more than one officer supposed to have credit with the Nawaub, but the slightest hint of the nature of his business seemed to strike all with terror. Not one of the persons he applied to would engage in the affair, or even consent to give it a hearing; and the Dewan plainly told him, that to engage in opposition to Prince Tippoo's wishes, was the ready way to destruction, and exhorted him to return to the coast. Driven almost to distraction by his various failures, Hartley betook himself in the evening to the Khan. The call of the Muezzins thundering from the minarets, had invited the faithful to prayers, when a black servant, about fifteen years old, stood before Hartley, and pronounced these words, deliberately, and twice over,—"Thus says Barak el Hadgi, the watcher in the Mosque: He that would see the sun rise, let him turn towards the east." He then left the caravanserai; and it may be well supposed that Hartley, starting from the carpet on which he had lain down to repose himself, followed his youthful guide with renewed vigour and palpitating hope.

CHAPTER 14

'Twas the hour when rites unholy
Call'd each Paynim voice to prayer,
And the star that faded slowly,
Left to dews the freshened air.

Day his sultry fires had wasted,
Calm and cool the moonbeams shone;
To the Vizier's lofty palace
One bold Christian came alone.

THOMAS CAMPBELL. *Quoted from memory.*

The twilight darkened into night so fast, that it was only by his white dress that Hartley could discern his guide, as he tripped along the splendid Bazaar of the city. But the obscurity was so far favourable, that it prevented the inconvenient attention which the natives might otherwise have bestowed upon the European in his native dress, a sight at that time very rare in Seringapatam.

The various turnings and windings through which he was conducted, ended at a small door in a wall, which, from the branches that hung over it, seemed to surround a garden or grove.

The postern opened on a tap from his guide, and the slave having entered, Hartley prepared to follow, but stepped back as a gigantic African brandished at his head a scimetar three fingers broad. The young slave touched his countryman with a rod which he held in his hand, and it seemed as if the touch disabled the giant, whose arm and weapon sunk instantly. Hartley entered without farther opposition, and was now in a grove of mango-trees, through which an infant moon was twinkling faintly amid the murmur of waters, the sweet song of the nightingale, and the odours of the rose, yellow jasmine, orange and citron flowers, and Persian narcissus. Huge domes and arches, which were seen imperfectly in the quivering light, seemed to intimate the neighbourhood of some sacred edifice, where the Fakir had doubtless taken up his residence.

140

Hartley pressed on with as much haste as he could, and entered a side-door and narrow vaulted passage, at the end of which was another door. Here his guide stopped, but pointed and made indications that the European should enter. Hartley did so, and found himself in a small cell, such as we have formerly described, wherein sate Barak el Hadgi, with another Fakir, who, to judge from the extreme dignity of a white beard, which ascended up to his eyes on each side, must be a man of great sanctity, as well as importance.

Hartley pronounced the usual salutation of Salam Alaikum in the most modest and deferential tone; but his former friend was so far from responding in their former strain of intimacy, that, having consulted the eye of his older companion, he barely pointed to a third carpet, upon which the stranger seated himself cross-legged, after the country fashion, and a profound silence prevailed for the space of several minutes. Hartley knew the Oriental customs too well to endanger the success of his suit by precipitation. He waited an intimation to speak. At length it came, and from Barak.

"When the pilgrim Barak," he said, "dwelt at Madras, he had eyes and a tongue; but now he is guided by those of his father, the holy Scheik Hali ben Khaledoun, the superior of his convent."

This extreme humility Hartley thought inconsistent with the affectation of possessing superior influence, which Barak had shown while at the Presidency; but exaggeration of their own consequence is a foible common to all who find themselves in a land of strangers. Addressing the senior Fakir, therefore, he told him in as few words as possible the villanous plot which was laid to betray Menie Gray into the hands of the Prince Tippoo. He made his suit for the reverend father's intercession with the Prince himself, and with his father the Nawaub, in the most persuasive terms. The Fakir listened to him with an inflexible and immovable aspect, similar to that with which a wooden saint regards his eager supplicants. There was a second pause, when, after resuming his pleading more than once, Hartley was at length compelled to end it for want of matter.

The silence was broken by the elder Fakir, who, after shooting a glance at his younger companion by a turn of the eye, without the least alteration of the position of the head and body, said, "The unbeliever has spoken like a poet. But does he think that the Nawaub Khan Hyder Ali Behauder will contest with his son Tippoo the victorious, the possession of an infidel slave?"

Hartley received at the same time a side glance from Barak, as if encouraging him to plead his own cause. He suffered a minute to elapse, and then replied,—

"The Nawaub is in the place of the Prophet, a judge over the low as well as high. It is written, that when the Prophet decided a controversy between the two sparrows concerning a grain of rice, his wife Fatima said to him, 'Doth the Missionary of Allah well to bestow his time in distributing justice on a matter so slight, and between such despicable litigants?'—'Know, woman,' answered the Prophet,'that the sparrows and the grain of rice are the creation of Allah. They are not worth more than thou hast spoken; but justice is a treasure of inestimable price, and it must be imparted by him who holdeth power to all who require it at his hand. The Prince doth the will of Allah, who gives it alike in small matters as in great, and to the poor as well as the powerful. To the hungry bird, a grain of rice is as a chaplet of pearls to a sovereign.'—I have spoken."

"Bismallah!—Praised be God! he hath spoken like a Moullah," said the elder Fakir, with a little more emotion, and some inclination of his head towards Barak, for on Hartley he scarcely deigned even to look.

"The lips have spoken it which cannot lie," replied Barak, and there was again a pause.

It was once more broken by Scheick Hali, who, addressing himself directly to Hartley, demanded of him, "Hast thou heard, Feringi, of aught of treason meditated by this Kafr [infidel] against the Nawaub Behander?"

"Out of a traitor cometh treason," said Hartley, "but, to speak after my knowledge, I am not conscious of such design."

"There is truth in the words of him," said the Fakir, "who accuseth not his enemy save on his knowledge. The things thou hast spoken shall be laid before the Nawaub; and as Allah and he will, so shall the issue be. Meantime, return to thy Khan, and prepare to attend the Vakeel of thy government, who is to travel with dawn to Bangalore, the strong, the happy, the holy city. Peace be with thee!—Is it not so, my son?"

Barak, to whom this appeal was made, replied, "Even as my father hath spoken."

Hartley had no alternative but to arise and take his leave with the usual phrase, "Salam—God's peace be with you!"

His youthful guide, who waited his return without, conducted him once more to his Khan, through by-paths which he could not have found out without pilotage. His thoughts were in the mean time strongly engaged on his late interview. He knew the Moslem men of religion were not implicitly to be trusted. The whole scene might be a scheme of Barak, to get rid of the trouble of patronizing a European in a delicate affair; and he determined to be guided by what should seem to confirm or discredit the intimation which he had received.

On his arrival at the Khan, he found the Vakeel of the British government in a great bustle, preparing to obey directions transmitted to him by the Nawaub's Dewan, or treasurer, directing him to depart the next morning with break of day for Bangalore.

He expressed great discontent at the order, and when Hartley intimated his purpose of accompanying him, seemed to think him a fool for his pains, hinting the probability that Hyder meant to get rid of them both by means of the freebooters, through whose countries they were to pass with such a feeble escort. This fear gave way to another, when the time of departure came, at which moment there rode up about two hundred of the Nawaub's native cavalry. The Sirdar who commanded these troops behaved with civility, and stated that he was directed to attend upon the travellers, and to provide for their safety and convenience on the journey; but his manner was reserved and distant, and the Vakeel insisted that the force was intended to prevent their escape, rather than for their protection. Under such unpleasant auspices, the journey between Seringapatam and Bangalore was accomplished in two days and part of a third, the distance being nearly eighty miles.

On arriving in view of this fine and populous city, they found an encampment already established within a mile of its walls. It occupied a tope or knoll, covered with trees, and looked full on the gardens which Tippoo had created in one quarter of the city. The rich pavilions of the principal persons flamed with silk and gold; and spears with gilded points, or poles supporting gold knobs, displayed numerous little banners inscribed with the name of the Prophet. This was the camp of the Begum Mootee Mahul, who, with a small body of her troops, about two hundred men, was waiting the return of Tippoo under the walls of Bangalore. Their private motives for desiring a meeting the reader is acquainted with; to the public the visit of the Begum had only the appearance of an act of deference, frequently paid by inferior and subordinate princes to the patrons whom they depend upon.

These facts ascertained, the Sirdar of the Nawaub took up his own encampment within sight of that of the Begum, but at about half a mile's distance, despatching to the city a messenger to announce to the Prince Tippoo, as soon as he should arrive, that he had come hither with the English Vakeel.

The bustle of pitching a few tents was soon over, and Hartley, solitary and sad, was left to walk under the shade of two or three mango-trees, and looking to the displayed streamers of the Begum's encampment, to reflect that amid these insignia of Mahomedanism Menie Gray remained, destined by a profligate and treacherous lover to the fate of slavery to a heathen tyrant. The consciousness of being in her vicinity added to the bitter pangs with which Hartley contemplated her situation, and reflected how little chance there appeared of his being able to rescue her from it by the mere force of reason and justice, which was all he could oppose to the selfish passions of a voluptuous tyrant. A lover of romance might have meditated some means of effecting her release by force or address; but Hartley, though a man of courage, had no spirit of adventure, and would have regarded as desperate any attempt of the kind.

His sole gleam of comfort arose from the impression which he had apparently made upon the elder Fakir, which he could not help hoping might be of some avail to him. But on one thing he was firmly resolved, and that was not to relinquish the cause he had engaged in whilst a grain of hope remained. He had seen in his own profession a quickening and a revival of life in the patient's eye, even when glazed apparently by the hand of Death; and he was taught confidence amidst moral evil by his success in relieving that which was physical only.

While Hartley was thus meditating, he was roused to attention by a heavy firing of artillery from the high bastions of the town; and turning his eyes in that direction, he could see advancing, on the northern side of Bangalore, a tide of cavalry, riding tumultuously forward, brandishing their spears in all different attitudes, and pressing their horses to a gallop. The clouds of dust which attended this vanguard, for such it was, combined with the smoke of the guns, did not permit Hartley to see distinctly the main body which followed; but the appearance of howdahed elephants and royal banners dimly seen through the haze, plainly intimated the return of Tippoo to Bangalore; while shouts, and irregular discharges of musketry, announced the real or pretended rejoicing of the inhabitants. The city gates received the living torrent, which rolled towards them; the clouds of smoke and dust were soon dispersed, and the horizon was restored to serenity and silence.

The meeting between persons of importance, more especially of royal rank, is a matter of very great consequence in India, and generally much address is employed to induce the person receiving the visit, to come as far as possible to meet the visitor. From merely rising up, or going to the edge of the carpet, to advancing to the gate of the palace, to that of the city, or, finally, to a mile or two on the road, is all subject to negotiation. But Tippoo's impatience to possess the fair European induced him to grant on this occasion a much greater degree of courtesy than the Begum had dared to expect, and he appointed his garden, adjacent to the city walls, and indeed included within the precincts of the fortifications, as the place of their meeting; the hour noon, on the day succeeding his arrival; for the natives seldom move early in the morning, or before having broken their fast. This was intimated to the Begum's messenger by the Prince in person, as, kneeling before him, he presented the *mizzar*, (a tribute consisting of three, five, or seven gold Mohurs, always an odd number,) and received in exchange a khelaut, or dress of honour. The messenger, in return, was eloquent in describing the importance of his mistress, her devoted veneration for the Prince, the pleasure which she experienced on the prospect of their motakul, or meeting, and concluded with a more modest compliment to his own extraordinary talents, and the confidence which the Begum reposed in him. He then departed; and orders were given that on the next day all should be in readiness for the *Sowarree*, a grand procession, when the Prince was to receive the Begum as his honoured guest at his pleasure-house in the gardens.

Long before the appointed hour, the rendezvous of Fakirs, beggars, and idlers, before the gate of the palace, intimated the excited expectations of those who usually attend processions; while a more urgent set of mendicants, the courtiers, were hastening thither, on horses or elephants, as their means afforded, always in a hurry to show their zeal, and with a speed proportioned to what they hoped or feared.

At noon precisely, a discharge of cannon, placed in the outer courts, as also of match-locks and of small swivels, carried by camels, (the poor animals shaking their long ears at every discharge,) announced that Tippoo had mounted his elephant. The solemn and deep sound of the naggra, or state drum, borne upon an elephant, was then heard like the distant discharge of artillery, followed by a long roll of musketry, and was instantly answered by that of numerous trumpets and tom-toms, (or common drums,) making a discordant, but yet a martial din. The noise increased as the procession traversed the outer courts of the palace in succession, and at length issued from the gates, having at their head the Chobdars, bearing silver sticks and clubs, and shouting, at the pitch of their voices, the titles and the virtues of Tippoo, the great, the generous, the invincible—strong as Rustan, just as Noushirvan—with a short prayer for his continued health.

After these came a confused body of men on foot, bearing spears, match-locks, and banners, and intermixed with horsemen, some in complete shirts of mail, with caps of steel under their turbans, some in a sort of defensive armour, consisting of rich silk dresses, rendered sabre proof by being stuffed with cotton. These champions preceded the Prince, as whose body guards they acted. It was not till after this time that Tippoo raised his celebrated Tiger-regiment, disciplined and armed according to the European fashion. Immediately before the Prince came, on a small elephant, A hard-faced, severe-looking man, by office the distributor of alms, which he flung in showers of small copper money among the Fakirs and beggars, whose scrambles to collect them seemed to augment their amount; while the grim-looking agent of Mahomedan charity, together with his elephant, which marched with half angry eyes, and its trunk curled upwards, seemed both alike ready to chastise those whom poverty should render too importunate.

Tippoo himself next appeared, richly apparelled, and seated on an elephant, which, carrying its head above all the others in the procession, seemed proudly conscious of superior dignity. The howdah, or seat which the Prince occupied, was of silver, embossed and gilt, having behind a place for a confidential servant, who waved the great chowry, or cow-tail, to keep off the flies; but who could also occasionally perform the task of spokesman, being well versed in all terms of flattery and compliment. The caparisons of the royal elephant were of scarlet cloth, richly embroidered with gold. Behind Tippoo came the various courtiers and officers of the household, mounted chiefly on elephants, all arrayed in their most splendid attire, and exhibiting the greatest pomp.

In this manner the procession advanced down the principal street of the town, to the gate of the royal gardens. The houses were ornamented by broad cloth, silk shawls, and embroidered carpets of the richest colours, displayed from the verandahs and windows; even the meanest hut was adorned with some piece of cloth, so that the whole street had a singularly rich and gorgeous appearance.

This splendid procession having entered the royal gardens, approached, through a long avenue of lofty trees, a chabootra, or platform of white marble, canopied by arches of the same material, which occupied the centre. It was raised four or five feet from the ground, covered with white cloth and Persian carpets. In the centre of the platform was the musnud, or state cushion of the prince, six feet square, composed of crimson velvet, richly embroidered. By special grace, a small low cushion was placed on the right of the Prince, for the occupation of the Begum. In front of this platform was a square tank, or pond of marble, four feet deep, and filled to the brim, with water as clear as crystal, having a large jet or fountain in the middle, which threw up a column of it to the height of twenty feet.

The Prince Tippoo had scarcely dismounted from his elephant, and occupied the musnod, or throne of cushions, when the stately form of the Begum was seen advancing to the place of rendezvous. The elephant being left at the gate of the gardens opening into the country, opposite to that by which the procession of Tippoo had entered, she was carried in an open litter, richly ornamented with silver, and borne on the shoulders of six black slaves. Her person was as richly attired as silks and gems could accomplish.

Richard Middlemas, as the Begum's General or Bukshee, walked nearest to her litter, in a dress as magnificent in itself as it was remote from all European costume, being that of a Banka, or Indian courtier. His turban was of rich silk and gold, twisted very hard and placed on one side of his head, its ends hanging down on the shoulder. His mustaches were turned and curled, and his eyelids stained with antimony. The vest was of gold brocade, with a cummerband, or sash, around his waist, corresponding to his turban. He carried in his hand a large sword, sheathed in a scabbard of crimson velvet, and wore around his middle a broad embroidered sword-belt. What thoughts he had under this gay attire, and the bold bearing which corresponded to it, it would be fearful to unfold. His least detestable hopes were perhaps those which tended to save Menie Gray, by betraying the Prince who was about to confide in him, and the Begum, at whose intercession Tippoo's confidence was to be reposed.

The litter stopped as it approached the tank, on the opposite side of which the Prince was seated on his musnud. Middlemas assisted the Begum to descend, and led her, deeply veiled with silver muslin, towards the platform of marble. The rest of the retinue of the Begum followed in their richest and most gaudy attire, all males, however; nor was there a symptom of woman being in her train, except that a close litter, guarded by twenty black slaves, having their sabres drawn, remained at some distance in a thicket of flowering shrubs.

When Tippoo Saib, through the dim haze which hung over the Waterfall, discerned the splendid train of the Begum advancing, he arose from his musnud, so as to receive her near the foot of his throne, and exchanged greetings with her upon the pleasure of meeting, and enquiries after their mutual health. He then conducted her to the cushion placed near to his own, while his courtiers anxiously showed their politeness in accommodating those of the Begum with places upon the carpets around, where they all sat down cross-legged—Richard Middlemas occupying a conspicuous situation.

The people of inferior note stood behind, and amongst them was the Sirdar of Hyder Ali, with Hartley and the Madras Vakeel. It would be impossible to describe the feelings with which Hartley recognized the apostate Middlemas and the Amazonian Mrs. Montreville. The sight of them worked up his resolution to make an appeal against them in full Durbar, to the justice which Tippoo was obliged to render to all who should complain of injuries. In the meanwhile, the Prince, who had hitherto spoken in a low voice, while acknowledging, it is to be supposed, the service and the fidelity of the Begum, now gave the sign to his attendant, who said, in an elevated tone, "Wherefore, and to requite these services, the mighty Prince, at the request of the mighty Begum, Mootee Mahul, beautiful as the moon, and wise as the daughter of Giamschid, had decreed to take into his service the Bukshee of her armies, and to invest him, as one worthy of all confidence, with the keeping of his beloved capital of Bangalore."

The voice of the crier had scarce ceased, when it was answered by one as loud, which sounded from the crowd of bystanders, "Cursed is he who maketh the robber Leik his treasurer, or trusteth the lives of Moslemah to the command of an apostate!"

With unutterable satisfaction, yet with trembling doubt and anxiety, Hartley traced the speech to the elder Fakir, the companion of Barak. Tippoo seemed not to notice the interruption, which passed for that of some mad devotee, to whom the Moslem princes permit great freedoms. The Durbar, therefore, recovered from their surprise; and, in answer to the proclamation, united in the shout of applause which is expected to attend every annunciation of the royal pleasure.

Their acclamation had no sooner ceased than Middlemas arose, bent himself before the musnud, and, in a set speech, declared his unworthiness of such high honour as had now been conferred, and his zeal for the Prince's service. Something remained to be added, but his speech faltered, his limbs shook, and his tongue seemed to refuse its office.

The Begum started from her seat, though contrary to etiquette, and said, as if to supply the deficiency in the speech of her officer, "My slave would say, that in acknowledgment of so great an honour conferred on my Bukshee, I am so void of means, that I can only pray your Highness will deign to accept a lily from Frangistan, to plant within the recesses of the secret garden of thy pleasures. Let my lord's guards carry yonder litter to the Zenana."

A female scream—was heard, as, at the signal from Tippoo, the guards of his seraglio advanced to receive the closed litter from the attendants of the Begum. The voice of the old Fakir was heard louder and sterner than before.—"Cursed is the Prince who barters justice for lust! He shall die in the gate by the sword of the stranger."

"This is too insolent!" said Tippoo. "Drag forward that Fakir, and cut his robe into tatters on his back with your chabouks."[14]

But a scene ensued like that in the hall of Seyd. All who attempted to obey the command of the incensed despot fell back from the Fakir, as they would from the Angel of Death. He flung his cap and fictitious beard on the ground, and the incensed countenance of Tippoo was subdued in an instant, when he encountered the stern and awful eye of his father. A sign dismissed him from the throne, which Hyder himself ascended, while the official menials hastily disrobed him of his tattered cloak, and flung on him a robe of regal splendour, and placed on his head a jewelled turban. The Durbar rung with acclamations to Hyder Ali Khan Behauder, "the good, the wise, the discoverer of hidden things, who cometh into the Divan like the sun bursting from the clouds."

The Nawaub at length signed for silence, and was promptly obeyed. He looked majestically around him, and at length bent his look upon Tippoo, whose downcast eyes, as he stood before the throne with his arms folded on his bosom, were strongly contrasted with the haughty air of authority which he had worn but a moment before. "Thou hast been willing," said the Nawaub, "to barter the safety of thy capital for the possession of a white slave. But the beauty of a fair woman caused Solomon ben David to stumble in his path; how much more, then, should the son of Hyder Naig remain firm under temptation!—That men may see clearly, we must remove the light which dazzles them. Yonder Feringi woman must be placed at my disposal."

"To hear is to obey," replied Tippoo, while the deep gloom on his brow showed what his forced submission cost his proud and passionate spirit. In the hearts of the courtiers present reigned the most eager curiosity to see the *denouement* of the scene, but not a trace of that wish was suffered to manifest

14 Long whips.

itself on features accustomed to conceal all internal sensations. The feelings of the Begum were hidden under her veil; while, in spite of a bold attempt to conceal his alarm, the perspiration stood in large drops on the brow of Richard Middlemas. The next words of the Nawaub sounded like music in the ear of Hartley.

"Carry the Feringi woman to the tent of the Sirdar Belash Cassim, [the chief to whom Hartley had been committed.] Let her be tended in all honour, and let him prepare to escort her, with the Vakeel and the Hakim Hartley, to the Payeen-Ghaut, [the country beneath the passes,] answering for their safety with his head." The litter was on its road to the Sirdar's tents ere the Nawaub had done speaking. "For thee, Tippoo," continued Hyder," I am not come hither to deprive thee of authority, or to disgrace thee before the Durbar. Such things as thou hast promised to this Feringi, proceed to make them good. The sun calleth not back the splendour which he lends to the moon; and the father obscures not the dignity which he has conferred on the son. What thou hast promised, that do thou proceed to make good."

The ceremony of investiture was therefore recommenced, by which the Prince Tippoo conferred on Middlemas the important government of the city of Bangalore, probably with the internal resolution, that since he was himself deprived of the fair European, he would take an early opportunity to remove the new Killedar from his charge; while Middlemas accepted it with the throbbing hope that he might yet outwit both father and son. The deed of investiture was read aloud—the robe of honour was put upon the newly created Killedar, and a hundred voices, while they blessed the prudent choice of Tippoo, wished the governor good fortune, and victory over his enemies.

A horse was led forward as the Prince's gift. It was a fine steed of the Cuttyawar breed, high-crested, with broad hind-quarters; he was of a white colour, but had the extremity of his tail and mane stained red. His saddle was red velvet, the bridle and crupper studded—with gilded knobs. Two attendants on lesser horses led this prancing animal, one holding the lance, and the other the long spear of their patron. The horse was shown to the applauding courtiers, and withdrawn in order to be led in state through the streets, while the new Killedar should follow on the elephant, another present usual on such an occasion, which was next made to advance, that the world might admire the munificence of the Prince.

The huge animal approached the platform, shaking his large wrinkled head, which he raised and sunk, as if impatient, and curling upwards his trunk from time to time, as if to show the gulf of his tongueless mouth. Gracefully retiring with the deepest obeisance, the Killedar, well pleased the audience was finished, stood by the neck of the elephant, expecting the conductor of the animal would make him kneel down, that he might ascend the gilded howdah, which awaited his occupancy.

"Hold, Feringi," said Hyder. "Thou hast received all that, was promised thee by the bounty of Tippoo. Accept now what is the fruit of the justice of Hyder."

As he spoke, he signed with his finger, and the driver of the elephant instantly conveyed to the animal the pleasure of the Nawaub. Curling his long trunk around the neck of the ill-fated European, the monster suddenly threw the wretch prostrate before him, and stamping his huge shapeless foot upon his breast, put an end at once to his life, and to his crimes. The cry which the victim uttered was mimicked by the roar of the monster, and a sound like an hysterical laugh mingling with a scream, which rung from under the veil of the Begum. The elephant once more raised his trunk aloft, and gaped fearfully.

The courtiers preserved a profound silence; but Tippoo, upon whose muslin robe a part of the victim's blood had spirted, held it up to the Nawaub, exclaiming in a sorrowful, yet resentful tone,—"Father—father—was it thus my promise should have been kept?"

"Know, foolish boy," said Hyder Ali, "that the carrion which lies there was in a plot to deliver Bangalore to the Feringis and the Mahrattas. This Begum [she started when she heard herself named] has given us warning of the plot, and has so merited her pardon for having originally concurred in it,—whether altogether out of love to us we will not too curiously enquire.—Hence with that lump of bloody clay, and let the Hakim Hartley and the English Vakeel come before me."

They were brought forward,—while some of the attendants flung sand upon the bloody traces, and others removed the crushed corpse.

"Hakim," said Hyder, "thou shalt return with the Feringi woman, and with gold to compensate her injuries,—wherein the Begum, as is fitting, shall contribute a share. Do thou say to thy nation, Hyder Ali acts justly." The Nawaub then inclined himself graciously to Hartley, and then turning to the Vakeel, who appeared much discomposed, "You have brought to me," he said, "words of peace,—while your masters meditated a treacherous war. It is not upon such as you that my vengeance ought to alight. But tell the Kafr [or infidel] Paupiah and his unworthy master, that Hyder Ali sees too clearly to suffer to be lost by treason the advantages he has gained by war. Hitherto I have been in the Carnatic as a mild Prince—in future I will be a destroying tempest! Hitherto I have made inroads as a compassionate and merciful conqueror—hereafter I will be the messenger whom Allah sends to the kingdoms which he visits in judgment!"

It is well known how dreadfully the Nawaub kept this promise, and how he and his son afterwards sunk before the discipline and bravery of the Europeans. The scene of just punishment which he so faithfully exhibited might be owing to his policy, his internal sense of right, and to the ostentation of displaying it before an Englishman of sense and intelligence, or to all of these motives mingled together—but in what proportions it is not for us to distinguish.

Hartley reached the coast in safety with his precious charge, rescued from a dreadful fate when she was almost beyond hope. But the nerves and constitution of Menie Gray had received a shock from which she long suffered severely, and never entirely recovered. The principal ladies of the settlement, moved by the singular tale of her distress, received her with the utmost kindness, and exercised towards her the most attentive and affectionate hospitality. The Nawaub, faithful to his promise, remitted to her a sum of no less than ten thousand gold Mohurs, extorted, as was surmised, almost entirely from the hoards of the Begum Mootee Mahul, or Montreville. Of the fate of that adventuress nothing was known for certainty; but her forts and government were taken into Hyder's custody, and report said, that, her power being abolished and her consequence lost, she died by poison, either taken by herself, or administered by some other person.

It might be thought a natural conclusion of the history of Menie Gray, that she should have married Hartley, to whom she stood much indebted for his heroic interference in her behalf. But her feelings were too much and too painfully agitated, her health too much shattered, to permit her to entertain thoughts of a matrimonial connexion, even with the acquaintance of her youth, and the champion of her freedom. Time might have removed these obstacles, but not two years, after their adventures in Mysore, the gallant and disinterested Hartley fell a victim to his professional courage, in withstanding the progress of a contagious distemper, which he at length caught, and under which he sunk. He left a considerable part of the moderate fortune which he had acquired to Menie Gray, who, of course, did not want for many advantageous offers of a matrimonial character. But she respected the memory of Hartley too much, to subdue in behalf of another the reasons which induced her to refuse the hand which he had so well deserved—nay, it may be thought, had so fairly won.

She returned to Britain—what seldom occurs—unmarried though wealthy; and, settling in her native village, appeared to find her only pleasure in acts of benevolence which seemed to exceed the extent of her fortune, had not her very retired life been taken into consideration. Two or three persons with whom she was intimate, could trace in her character that generous and disinterested simplicity and affection, which were the ground-work of her character. To the world at large her habits seemed those of the ancient Roman matron, which is recorded on her tomb in these four words,

DOMUM MANSIT—LANAM FECIT.

MR. CROFTANGRY'S CONCLUSION

If you tell a good jest,
And please all the rest,
Comes Dingley, and asks you, "What was it?"
And before she can know,
Away she will go
To seek an old rag in the closet.

DEAN SWIFT.

While I was inditing the goodly matter which my readers have just perused, I might be said to go through a course of breaking-in to stand criticism, like a shooting-pony to stand fire. By some of those venial breaches of confidence, which always take place on the like occasions, my private flirtations with the Muse of Fiction became a matter whispered in Miss Fairscribe's circle, some ornaments of which were, I suppose, highly interested in the progress of the affair, while others "really thought Mr. Chrystal Croftangry might have had more wit at his time of day." Then came the sly intimation, the oblique remark, all that sugar-lipped raillery which is fitted for the situation of a man about to do a foolish thing, whether it be to publish or to marry, and that accompanied with the discreet nods and winks of such friends as are in the secret, and the obliging eagerness of others to know all about it.

At length the affair became so far public, that I was induced to face a tea-party with my manuscript in my pocket, looking as simple and modest as any gentleman of a certain age need to do upon such an occasion. When tea had been carried round, handkerchiefs and smelling bottles prepared, I had the honour of reading the Surgeon's Daughter for the entertainment of the evening. It went off excellently; my friend Mr. Fairscribe, who had been seduced from his desk to join the literary circle, only fell asleep twice, and readily recovered his attention by help of his snuff-box. The ladies were politely attentive, and when the cat, or the dog, or a next neighbour, tempted an individual to relax, Katie Fairscribe was on the alert, like an active whipper-in, with look, touch, or whisper, to recall them to a sense of what was going

on. Whether Miss Katie was thus active merely to enforce the literary discipline of her coterie, or whether she was really interested by the beauties of
the piece, and desirous to enforce them on others, I will not venture to ask, in
case I should end in liking the girl—and she is really a pretty one. Better than
wisdom would warrant, either for my sake or hers.

I must own, my story here and there flagged a good deal; perhaps there
were faults in my reading, for while I should have been attending to nothing
but how to give the words effect as they existed, I was feeling the chilling
consciousness, that they might have been, and ought to have been, a great
deal better. However, we kindled up at last when we got to the East Indies,
although on the mention of tigers, an old lady, whose tongue had been impatient for an hour, broke in with, "I wonder if Mr. Croftangry ever heard the
story of Tiger Tullideph?" and had nearly inserted the whole narrative as an
episode in my tale. She was, however, brought to reason, and the subsequent
mention of shawls, diamonds, turbans, and cummerbands, had their usual
effect in awakening the imaginations of the fair auditors. At the extinction of
the faithless lover in a way so horribly new, I had, as indeed I expected, the
good fortune to excite that expression of painful interest which is produced by
drawing in the breath through the compressed lips; nay, one Miss of fourteen
actually screamed.

At length my task was ended, and the fair circle rained odours upon me,
as they pelt beaux at the Carnival with sugar-plums, and drench them with
scented spices. There was "Beautiful," and "Sweetly interesting," and "O Mr.
Croftangry," and "How much obliged," and "What a delightful evening," and
"O Miss Katie, how could you keep such a secret so long?" While the dear
souls were thus smothering me with rose leaves, the merciless old lady carried
them all off by a disquisition upon shawls, which she had the impudence to
say, arose entirely out of my story. Miss Katie endeavoured to stop the flow
of her eloquence in vain; she threw all other topics out of the field, and from
the genuine Indian, she made a digression to the imitation shawls now made
at Paisley, out of real Thibet wool, not to be known from the actual Country
shawl, except by some inimitable cross-stitch in the border. "It is well," said
the old lady, wrapping herself up in a rich Kashmire, "that there is some way
of knowing a thing that cost fifty guineas from an article that is sold for five;
but I venture to say there are not one out of ten thousand that would understand the difference."

The politeness of some of the fair ladies would now have brought back
the conversation to the forgotten subject of our meeting. "How could you,
Mr. Croftangry, collect all these hard words about India?—you were never
there?"—"No, madam, I have not had that advantage; but, like the imitative
operatives of Paisley, I have composed my shawl by incorporating into the
woof a little Thibet wool, which my excellent friend and neighbour, Colonel

Mackerris, one of the best fellows who ever trode a Highland moor, or dived into an Indian jungle, had the goodness to supply me with."

My rehearsal, however, though not absolutely and altogether to my taste, has prepared me in some measure for the less tempered and guarded sentence of the world. So a man must learn to encounter a foil before he confronts a sword; and to take up my original simile, a horse must be accustomed to a *feu de joie*, before you can ride him against a volley of balls. Well, Corporal Nym's philosophy is not the worst that has been preached, "Things must be as they may." If my lucubrations give pleasure, I may again require the attention of the courteous reader; if not, here end the

CHRONICLES OF THE CANONGATE.

www.ingramcontent.com/pod-product-compliance
Lightning Source LLC
Chambersburg PA
CBHW071301130626
46556CB00003B/1418